THE SHADOW
OF SALT CREST

DAZE EVANDER

THE SHADOW: OF SALT CREST

ISBN-13: 979-8-9854845-9-5 (Paperback)

ISBN-13: 979-8-9901045-0-1 (Hardback)

ISBN-13: 979-8-9901045-1-8 (eBook)

Library of Congress Control Number: 2024903944

Published by Faction Realm Press

www.factionrealmpress.com

INTRODUCTION:

When welcoming someone to Salt Crest City, it's crucial to first introduce the main groups of the Frontier on what they wear and wield:

1. **Emergency Biohazard** (In Gray/Use Guns)
2. **Experiment Sciences** (In Purple/Use Swords)

A divide formed after testing went wrong. Nearly all the employees tried to quit after the tragedies, but contractual agreements bound them to the agency for a certain number of years—determined by merit or bribery. Everyone signed non-disclosure agreements, and their uniforms were changed, the colors gray and purple now separating them into two distinct groups.

After the disaster rendered an oasis hazardous, a sanction was written. Teams of detectives saw an opportunity to conduct experiments far off the grid, and they seized it. However, their mud-covered tests were not yielding results. When things got out of hand, they decided to get rid of the remains, starting a countdown on a magnetic force designed to wipe out the literary texts—and inhabitants—of Salt Crest City...

– Those who knew too much

CONTENTS

Title Page

Copyright

Introduction

List of Acknowledgements:

Chapter One: City Lights...1

Chapter Two: Stained Paragraphs.....................25

Chapter Three: Side Mission.............................54

Chapter Four: Tape Recordings......................68

Chapter Five: Medkit...88

Chapter Six: Trust Fall....................................109

Chapter Seven: An Open Book......................128

Chapter Eight: Eyebright...............................154

Chapter Nine: Tunnel Maze...........................176

Chapter Ten: Sequence...................................199

Chapter Eleven: Last Sight............................222

Chapter Twelve: Switching Sides.................235

Chapter Thirteen: Past Events.......................258

Chapter Fourteen: Wielders of Magic...........280

Novel Extra: Character Poems.......................309

LIST OF ACKNOWLEDGEMENTS:

All
Art By:

JAMES CHILD

Series
Editor:

MICHAELA DELANEY
The Wordsmith Editorial

**I'm grateful for you,
for all of your hard work and
amazing talent.**

**Thank you so much to everyone supporting me.
To all of my friends, family, and the love of my
life: I love you - this story is here because of you.**
Storytelling is my favorite thing to do and this one
is inspired by many that are close to my heart.
I'm so thankful for those who have helped
bring this title to life and your encouragement
means more than I can ever put into words.
I hope you will enjoy this new journey.

- DAZE EVANDER

ZEKIEL

Evening-Night-Morning

72 hours remaining

CHAPTER ONE: CITY LIGHTS

WHEN BETTER BECOMES WORSE IT'S TIME TO get away, even if that means stepping into the unknown. I believed that was where I belonged—as far away from magic, and anyone who used it, as possible. It felt as though only the good things came to an end, while everything else just continued. My past was filled with loss, and magic, intrinsically woven together by memories that had been seared into my mind. They became challenging to separate. The other thing I wanted to leave behind was the version of myself that still had hope. Only a severe and permanent removal could get me away from it all—stepping off into a void. I thought that returning there would lead me to a state of blissful unawareness, where I wouldn't feel the pain of loss...

I was wrong. I had been wrong about many things.

As I stepped into the oceanside portal on the mysterious, magical planet I longed to escape from, it filled with stars. It sounded like a broken vacuum—the same noise I'd heard once before—and after an uncomfortable landing, I emerged on the other side. The first thing I noticed was the slimy mud beneath my hands and feet. With an aching neck, I gathered what little strength I had to look up and saw a dreary, unfamiliar place stretching out before me. The storm clouds above mirrored the deep gray shades of the mud. I anxiously turned around, hoping to go back and live in the past instead, but the portal had vanished.

My hands dripped with sweat as I tried to forget what I once had done with them in combat. As I nervously ran them over my arms and legs, I no longer felt any trace of my magical past. My body seemed to have returned to its natural state.

I almost lost my footing, slipping slightly against the mud, as I ventured toward the white blobs in the distance. The bulk of the wasteland was mostly mud and water, with only a small portion of it taken up by a city. It seemed to be evening when I arrived, though the sun could barely be seen setting and there were no stars in the sky. Surrounded by an endless gray, I continued forward and tried to keep a steady balance.

Suppressing what felt like recent memories was difficult. I tried not to think of those I had been close to and lost—their lives tragically taken while fighting with magic—and the ones who were still alive that I cared for yet walked away from. I had to push onward despite the lingering sorrow—to forgive myself. *They'd want me to keep going, wouldn't they? If only I could talk to her right now. She always knew exactly what to say.* I shouldn't be surprised if forever didn't last yet again.

The clothes I had worn for a while were weathered from rain, sand, and dirt. My hair was unkempt, my lips chapped, and I yearned for a drink of water as I left a trail of weary footsteps in the mud. Despite the gloomy atmosphere, the air was getting hotter with each second, making the small amount of flannel fabric I had on feel unbearably uncomfortable.

There was only the sound of the wind until I reached the front gates. Twenty thick, gunmetal-gray sections wrapped around the perimeter, with white light beaming from glowing signs. Withering vines wove through the alleyways and crumbling walls.

As I approached the sturdy entrance doors, warm droplets of rain fell around me. I was met by a group of armored strangers who quickly ushered me inside, barely speaking and casting worried glances around. To my side, a large, dusty sign displayed the name SALT CREST CITY.

I pushed away the uncomfortable memories of my past that reminded me of who I used to be. *I can't think like this. Not anymore. I could have a fresh start here, I could move on.* Yet, guilt and sadness wrestled for my attention, and a knot grew in my empty stomach.

I almost fell victim to my head again as I refrained from scolding myself for overthinking, desperately trying to remain hopeful for a new beginning.

For miles around the city, there was nothing but mud.

It was cluttered with worn-out and random items—old doors, mailboxes with bullet holes, dressers, bed frames. Almost everything looked to be destroyed and abandoned for many years. Most of it had been damaged and corroded away into scattered pieces.

At the heart of the city stood a cement core, around which others walked. However, as it grew darker, many of them started to leave.

The ruins of abandoned items were used to section off spaces. Large, rusted sheets served as roofs, old RV campers were stacked on top of one another while accompanied by painted ladders, and bulbs of neon lights had been strung around hanging wires. Overstuffed bins filled with scrap and trash were around many corners.

Most of the walls were corroding away, trunks stored worn-out weaponry and miscellaneous parts, and people sat idly by in gum-covered alleyways. The predominant pigment of their clothing was purple, followed by gray, with some dressed entirely in black.

As I walked further inside, a small, wrecked wooden ship caught my eye, and there was a glow from a light flickering overhead. *I need to find out more about this place's history.* A few empty bottles had been stuck onto the shards of pointy wood, and I read the label on one of them.

SB DRINKS

Several buildings faced each other in a certain order, mostly guarded by strangers in dark gray leather armor.

<table>
<tr><td>WEAPONS</td><td>DINING</td></tr>
<tr><td>ARMORY</td><td>RESIDING</td></tr>
<tr><td>SEA BARTERING</td><td>TRAINING</td></tr>
<tr><td>STORAGE</td><td>CROW LIBRARY</td></tr>
<tr><td>LOOT VAULTS</td><td>CELL BLOCK</td></tr>
</table>

I came upon the weapons shop first and took in the many guns that were on display. While there were mostly pistols and shotguns, it was the swords hanging on the back wall that truly caught my eye. Curved blades had futuristic shapes, and some handles were branded with particular symbols like quills and clouds in the leather. I couldn't decide which one I liked the best, as each had something unique about it. A gold one, in particular, caught my attention. It rested up against the counter, seemingly within reach of visitors.

I ran my tired fingers over the handle and noticed an infinity symbol discreetly pressed into it. There was hardly anyone else shopping while I searched around for some sort of price. *This would probably come in handy—who knows what lives out here? There must be a reason why they have all this gear.*

"I already told you, Tule, I'm not interested in listening to those tapes," said a short individual, who appeared to be the shop owner, as he stepped inside from the crowded walkway. "It all sounds like Euphrasia Arms is trying to stir up false propaganda to boost their sales."

Someone followed after the man in gray, and I stilled when my eyes found her. "With all due respect... that isn't the case. I could explain them to you in more detail if you'd like?"

"Maybe another time, alright?" He let out a sigh.

She gave him a polite smile and then looked over at me. *Tule.* I repeated her name in my mind as I saw her heading my way.

"I'm sorry you had to hear that." Her hands were filled with books covered in ashy notes and what seemed to be vintage tape recorders.

I gave an understanding nod. *No worries at all.*

"You're new here, right? Haven't seen you before." She looked me up and down.

I nodded again.

"It takes time for skepticism to wear off after someone new shows up. You're guilty until proven innocent, especially with what is at stake." She shifted her items to offer me her hand. "I'm Tule."

"Zekiel."

Her dark curls cascaded onto a purple suit of armor, which had been modified with sharp metal jutting out from her shoulders and ankles. Small paintings of flowers adorned each of her wrists.

"I can show you around the city if you'd like?" she offered.

"I would appreciate that greatly, thank you," I replied, momentarily struck by the genuine warmth of her smile.

I struggled to keep up as she gave me a tour of the city. Sweat dripped from my forehead in the heat, made worse by the long strands of hair hanging over my face. I didn't ask many questions as we walked, passing through areas filled with trash and discarded items. Rusty nails and metal scraps were scattered on the ground, remnants of others modifying their weapons and armor.

"There seems to be a dress code," I said quietly to myself after observing the repetitive patterns of attire.

Nearby, five strangers stood proudly in matching gray outfits. They were illuminated not only by the white lights but also the rising moon, which was just beginning to creep up over the twelve main buildings. Nightfall had arrived quickly. As we kept walking, an unsettling horn began to blare.

"That's a warning if someone shows up and the staff needs to do one last perimeter sweep to ensure everyone is safe," Tule explained. "You must remember not to wander past the gates once the moon rises. When it does, all that mud you were walking on turns into an endless ocean. No one has ever tried to swim in it because something lurks below—a dragon. I've seen its scaly back peek out from the waters at times during the night, it sleeps while it is daytime."

I assumed we were nearing our destination as Tule slowed her pace, either to guide me more carefully or to help me keep up despite my fatigue.

Many of the appliances around us were missing screws and looked as though they might topple over if someone leaned on them—especially the sparse and dirty trash cans, which had been rummaged through the most.

Tule looked up at me and said, "Not much of the unknown has been seen, as no one has ever gotten close to it. There have been no reported deaths, at least not from what is found in the light. Skeletons might be buried in the darkness."

"What planet are we on?" I asked, looking around. *I have to get my bearings.*

"Earth," she replied, "I'm trying to locate our exact coordinates. No one has ventured far enough to see what else can be found beyond the horizon. Well, people from the *past* have." She excitedly showed me the collection of books and tape recorders she was carrying. "I'm planning to broadcast a message through the Sea Bartering shop's outside speakers about a poisonous mist that's on the way. There's a cure, and it's very important that we find it." She paused, her eyes flashing with determination. "Unfortunately, many of the people here don't believe that what I'm saying will happen. They want to ban the books we have and ignore the clues of magic they give us."

I stayed quiet for a moment, processing what she had said. "I'd like to learn more about what you have here."

Tule stopped in her tracks, her eyes widening in surprise. "Hardly anyone I've met has wanted to. Are you serious?"

"I tend to be," I replied quietly, my voice earnest.

She quickened her pace. "Great! Let's go talk in my quarters." We continued through the rain, avoiding puddles and dodging the other citygoers who walked around aimlessly. The structural integrity of each dull building was poor, as if they could crumble at any moment.

I was growing lightheaded, desperate for sustenance, and I couldn't remember the last time I'd had a proper night's sleep either. Each breath felt drier than the one before. A few signs caught my eye, warning against drinking unfiltered water and reminding us that food was scarce. The city had scheduled ration days.

I almost sighed in relief when we reached Tule's place, which was nestled in between several rooms on the first story—which was probably the most convenient level. The blinds in the front window had been left open, revealing piles of her belongings stacked haphazardly inside.

"Are there only two types of weapons to choose from? It looks like everyone here is either armed with a gun or a sword." I nodded toward the impressive blade sheathed on her back.

"Yeah," Tule shrugged. "You could say that."

As I glanced away from her, I noticed a wooden door painted with white flowers. Drawn by their unique style, I stepped closer. *These match the ones on her armor. Must be a painter.* A large paintbrush and stacked cans sat by her doorstep, with splashes of yellow and purple, and outlines of petals waiting to be filled in. She used every inch of wood and metal as her canvas.

"Always watch your back," she suggested.

"You don't need to tell me that." *Trust me.*

I pushed memories of the past away as she unlocked the door and ushered me inside. Tule had crammed the small space with as many items as possible. There wasn't one empty shelf in sight. Every drawer was stuffed to the brim, stuck shut from the sheer volume of items she'd collected. *These had probably been tossed from workbenches or discarded.*

Charming that she holds onto what others likely think is just junk.

"Please make yourself comfortable while I get you a drink," Tule said, motioning to a lopsided chair. I took a seat as she emptied her things onto a nearby desk.

Dim light seeped into the kitchen before she closed the curtains. Dust fell from the woven fabric, settling on the few bread loaves on the counter. Beside them were clear, round jars of butter. She lit a cluster of candles and poured water into two cracked cups. The bin was nearly empty, but she made sure I was given a generous cup regardless.

The sound of wind whistled past the walls in a chilling tone. I glanced curiously at the drink on the table and waited for her to take a sip to see her reaction to it, despite my desperate thirst.

Tule sat in front of me, her expression serious yet inviting. "What would you like to discuss first?" she asked.

"Tell me more about the poison, please," I replied.

She leaned forward intensely. "We don't have much time. I've been studying literature from the library we passed by earlier, the building with the crow statue in front of it. A lot of symbolism incorporates the color green. It prophesied that a storm is coming... one we can't run from."

Doesn't sound good. I frowned with concern. "What did the forewarnings entail?" *I need to make sure I ask about getting a sword.*

She hesitated for a moment before speaking softly, a flicker of fear crossing her face. "The sky cracking like a glass ceiling with a poisonous mist."

"What clues have there been towards a cure?"

"Something from nature, but I'm not sure what," Tule admitted. "That's been my main focus lately as I've been trying to figure out our next steps."

"May I see one of the books? Who wrote them?" I inquired.

After clearing her throat, she took a swig of water before moving to an uneven coffee table. She grabbed a stack of books and set them down one by one, the motion causing ripples in my water.

"I'm not sure who wrote most of these, as they kept their identities a secret for some reason," Tule explained. "However, there's one author in particular who wrote a significant portion of what's on those shelves. I recommend starting with this one—it's quite interesting," she said, handing me a book.

It was nearly nine hundred pages long, and my wrists buckled under its weight. "Is this fictional?" I asked, noticing some tears and holes in it.

"I thought it was fiction at first, but now I'm not so sure," Tule said.

A chill ran down my spine as I paused, my unease growing. "Wait... what makes you say that?"

Tule didn't answer immediately. Instead, she watched me as I inspected the book, her fingers tapping lightly on the table. The edges of the pages looked as if they had been fed into a paper shredder but were pulled out just before the blades tore through each margin. The paper's sides were sprayed with gold, matching a border wrapped around the book's cover.

The title read: "*Crow Library's Tunnels.*" Its dust jacket featured an eerie, abstract depiction of the woods. The author concealed their identity with a simple:

-Anonymous

None of the chapters were named or numbered; instead, each began with a different symbol. *I really don't want to get involved with any of this.* Tule waited silently for me to share my thoughts, peering at the book and over to my disheveled hair, which flickered in the candlelight. *How do I tell her that I'm not willing to deal with anything regarding magic?*

"Why'd you want me to start with this one?" I asked, peering at her with curiosity.

"Sometimes books hold hidden keys," Tule replied, practically skipping to my side of the wobbly table. She leaned in closer. "Want to see something magical?"

I nodded, though it felt like I was going to whether I said yes or not.

She pulled away the dust jacket to reveal a plain gray cloth binding, then flipped the book onto its back, uncovering a map with a giant X marking a spot in a tangled forest. Her sweaty fingertip traced a glossy cluster of trees.

"There's something here that the story alludes to. The chapters are like puzzle pieces we need to put together. Time is already running out; the countdown of seventy-two hours has begun," Tule explained, her brown eyes shining with urgency.

"That sounds like a lot to process," I replied, feeling dizzy from the heat and exhaustion. "Maybe I can take this with me to read later? What do you suggest I do tomorrow?"

"Gear up. There's not much I wear besides this," she said, motioning to her outfit. "How about I show you where you'll be staying? You must be really tired. I'll keep an eye out and let you know if anything unusual happens."

"Sounds like a plan. I'd really enjoy a night's rest."

Tule led me out of her place and through the crowded residential area until we stopped at the third building. The doors were mismatched, with large chips of paint peeling away. Graffiti covered the walls, and many of the tables and dressers were damaged or unassembled. She guided me up a few flights of stairs to an unoccupied room. After a few loud knocks on a faded green door with no reply, she pulled out a ring of keys.

"I'm going to check something before you sleep," she said, pulling a pack of matches from her chest pocket and lighting one of the dresser candles.

Dust covered the floorboards, windowsill, and the broken fan hanging from the brittle ceiling. Tule checked beneath the stained mattress pad.

"I'm just making sure the bedding is in decent condition. Others have contracted illnesses from sleeping on them," she explained.

I waited in silence while she searched.

"This one looks okay," she said, staying crouched for a moment before pulling out a combat knife from under the bedding. "Found a free weapon for you. Hopefully, you won't need it soon. I hope you sleep well tonight."

"Thanks. You too," I said, mentally noting that I'd need to get a proper weapon as soon as possible.

Tule lingered for a moment, and we shared a quiet look. Though I had just met her, I didn't want to part ways. I smiled at her for the first time in a while, and she slowly left the room. The last thing I saw was her curls bouncing as she closed the door.

The next very warm morning, I took some time for myself in my new living quarters before heading out to get armor tailored. Despite enjoying being alone, I looked forward to meeting up with Tule again. I had shaved and trimmed my hair above my shoulders, leaving a few strands to sway loosely. *I can't believe that all of this is happening right now.* The shop's walls showcased old newspaper headlines behind broken glass frames:

RIVER BURST!

&

HAVOC ON OASIS!

Tule was already waiting for me when I arrived, giving me another smile. Her presence was reassuring, a stark contrast to the chaotic atmosphere of the shop.

The store offered a variety of armor options. The owner explained that each piece of leather was handcrafted by city members, with some created out of boredom and never used. Many of the designs incorporated sharp pieces of scrap metal into the armor's frame and connective components. I selected the heavy combat option to wear before changing out of my damaged attire in the fitting room.

In the corner, there was a mirror that looked just like the one I had in the bedroom I grew up in. For the first time, I didn't feel upset about how my hair or nose looked when I saw my reflection.

I'll figure out what's going on here, and I'll survive whatever comes my way. I just hope it won't involve magic.

The snug clothes I'd put on made me sweat more, and my boots thumped loudly as I walked back to speak with Tule. The sun's glow cast a warm light on my path as I passed a group of women admiring me. They smiled and whispered among themselves as I glanced their way, the orangish tones of the sun's warmth bouncing off my skin. I tried to adjust my posture, feeling a mix of self-consciousness and resolve.

"What do you think?" I asked Tule as I approached her, the ladies watching us from nearby.

I wore dark brown armor adorned with rocky metals and stones. The premium leather protected my arms, legs, and torso but left my chest exposed. I wiped the sweat from my forehead and put on an additional piece to cover the vulnerable areas. A long, dark navy-blue cloak, tailored to fit around my weapon holders, completed the set and matched my pants.

"It suits you," Tule said, yet she seemed to be worried. "You're not wearing any gray or purple."

"It took extra time to find this buried in the bins." The air around us was becoming stiflingly hot, making it harder to breathe. My lungs felt tight and my airways constricted. It was a struggle to talk. "How hot is it?"

She, too, was covered in sweat. "Very. It's always like this here. It's been this way since I arrived a while ago."

"Wow, it's just, like, *really* warm... you know?"

"Your armor is probably heavy—"

I suddenly felt a rush of blood to my head, accompanied by a sharp, thumping pain, and then I collapsed onto the hard floor.

"Zekiel! Are you okay? Did you just pass out?"

Tule cradled my face in her hands as smoke seemed to seep from my own fingers. For a few minutes, it felt as if the leather armor I had just donned was fusing with my sweaty skin. *What does this mean?* I was at a loss for words, watching in disbelief as a purple mist faded between my aching fingers. *Please don't tell me my magic is back! I can't endure those changes again!*

"What's going on?" someone asked from behind us, their voice edged with worry.

Another gasped. "Wait... is he one of *them*?"

A small crowd of strangers began to form around me.

"This can't be good," someone muttered, throwing up their hands.

"Here we go again with magic," another voice complained.

The crowd's murmurs grew chaotic, voices overlapping as they rolled their eyes. I could barely make out Tule's words as she leaned closer while I remained on the floor.

"This will probably cause a panic. Don't worry, I'll try to take care of things, okay?" she said reassuringly. "Just please keep quiet about your past. Let me manage the situation."

My heart raced again as Tule stayed close. "Okay," I managed to say. *How much does she know about where I came from?*

"Do something with them! Your hands!" a stranger demanded from the corner of the room.

"I can't. I don't have, or use magic, alright?" I protested.

A few groans erupted, and some of the onlookers walked away, while others stayed, their expressions judgmental and their arms crossed.

"Time to share warnings about supernatural spells making a comeback," one person said. "I told you it wasn't coming from somewhere but from *someone*."

"Yeah, yeah, yeah. Save the 'I told you so's' for later," the woman in gray snapped back. "For now, we'll just avoid him too."

"We need to let Castin know."

"Already on it." Those words were punctuated by a small beep as she tucked an unknown device into her pocket.

Tule helped me off the ground. "Let's get out of here before he starts asking questions."

Just then, the shop's doors swung open, and a rush of hot air and dust swirled around us, causing everyone to cough. Standing in the doorway was a man dressed entirely in gray. His oversized boots and short sleeves revealed numerous tattoos, including painted guns on his limbs, and a large hat obscured most of his face, which seemed twisted into a scowl.

"Where's the Magic Wielder at?" he demanded.

CASTIN

Afternoon-Evening

CHAPTER TWO: STAINED PARAGRAPHS

WORKING FOR THOSE I ONCE HID FROM WAS the solution—they would never suspect that any of the nuclear aftermath from the biennial tragedy had anything to do with me. I did my best to project a strong opposition to magic and the people, and forces, involved with it. As one of the commanding chiefs of our Emergency Biohazard unit, specializing in toxic waste and lethal chemical cleanup, I made sure to keep my supernatural experiences in the darkness. Instead, I directed my focus toward my years spent in an engineering firm or on the Frontier, hoping to keep any incriminating evidence away from scrutiny.

"I knew it was only a matter of time until yet another shady lawbreaker stepped through one of the sacred portals," I drawled.

"Word spreads faster than diseases around here!" someone proclaimed behind me as I entered the shop.

I continued, "I was working out and got interrupted with the news of someone unlawfully tampering with magic again."

"Those were just rumors," Tule said, glancing at me while helping the stranger to his feet. A wisp of smoke lingered around their hands, and I couldn't discern the spell he had cast.

"Getting in trouble here is serious business," I reminded her, stepping past a few of my crew members in gray. "How about you properly introduce yourself?"

"My name is Zekiel," he said, glaring through his disheveled hair.

"You'll need to explain how you arrived in this city," I said, scanning him from head to toe. "Not just anyone is allowed here. What group do you belong to? I can't tell from your attire."

"I'm not associated with either. I stepped through a portal and ended up here," he said, his tone defiant. "There's not much more I can tell you, but what I will say is that I refuse to be interrogated."

I reached outward for a handshake. "Nice to meet you."

He declined the gesture, keeping his head low.

"Alright then." I pulled out my work badge and flashed it at him. Though I doubted he'd recognize the high-ranking symbol, I had to adhere to standard protocol. "By law of the Frontier, you're required to disclose any past and present affiliations with magic, specifically F.E.M."

"What is that?" he asked, confusion evident in his voice.

Tule quickly gave him a worried look.

"You haven't told him yet?" I asked, my tone incredulous. "That should've been the first thing you learned about. Forced Evolutionary Magic. It's the worst kind—creates all sorts of messes that we in gray have to clean up. Right?"

The familiar faces around me nodded in agreement, murmuring their own experiences to back up my claims.

Ezra, my trusty comrade, spoke up the loudest. "I *told* you all earlier that he was probably a Magic Wielder."

"You were right," I said, addressing Zekiel as if he weren't right there with us. "They're exactly who we were warned about. Watch how everything will soon fall apart because of their never-ending curses."

I couldn't have spoken at a more opportune moment. A deep vibration shook the city's core. Everything tipped side to side, and I gripped the nearest grimy counter to keep my balance as unsecured items in the shop's displays toppled to the floor and shattered.

"The dragon's awake!" multiple voices exclaimed.

Wonder why it's up so early? It's like the creature sensed something nearby. Something in use. Such as... the legendary item! But it can't be. How could a newcomer have already acquired it before me?

"Look man, I don't even know *half* of what you're talking about," Zekiel said, his frustration clear. "How about you ease off?"

Ignoring him, I continued to look out of the window. "It's as if it wants something. Circling around like it's hunting. A valuable item might be close."

As I peered outside, I saw another newcomer sprint past the shop. Her braids flew behind her in the wind. She looked like she was hiding something. I knew the city's layout like the back of my hand and was familiar with the shortcut routes for back alley deals and magical gatherings. *I'm sure she's going to end up at the vaults. Every lawbreaker takes a chance to check for the hidden key there. Unless...* Then a different suspicion dawned on me. *What if it's not Zekiel who has it but instead the woman who just ran by? I have to follow her!*

"I'll speak with you all later," I said, leaving the group behind.

I always carried more than one gun, regardless of the time or circumstance. Salt Crest City was a place where you could never be too safe. The only thing that outnumbered the types of swords was the myriad of creative ways people could stab you in the back with them.

Typically, I avoided those who wielded swords, especially those in purple. But I was often reminded that those in black carried them as well.

Then I was on the heels of the woman headed straight for the Loot Vaults, just as I'd suspected.

My favorite pistol was gripped in my hand, fitted with an expensive suppressor and high-capacity magazine. I jogged in a wide circle around the cement core, navigating the narrow, precarious alleyways in pursuit of her.

I slowed as she finally reached the vaults, curious about her intentions. *Today won't be the first that I walk into or fall for a trap.* The secretive woman seemed to sense my presence momentarily, but I ensured she couldn't spot me by placing a magically charged grip on my weighty hat.

This headpiece was enchanted to render me invisible to others as long as I held onto it. Over time, I'd leveled up its powers, learning to cast invisibility not just for myself but also for anyone I chose during that duration. Still, I made sure to stay in shape at the training arena. I knew I had to also be sharp with my aim at all times.

The ground stopped shaking as she came to a halt, nervously tapping her foot on the concrete. I reminded myself to use every word carefully, looking down at my tattoos. Each one marked a skill I had mastered in combat, a reminder that silence could be as powerful as any weapon.

I started the conversation off simply, "You know that no one has ever been inside these vaults, right?"

She spun around, her startled eyes meeting mine as I walked towards her. "I was just looking. Hold on, I don't think we've met?"

I'd seen her face before. The familiarity struck me deeply, and when our eyes locked, it was as though I'd already studied her complex demeanor. Her deep brown ones seemed oddly familiar, even as I scrutinized her.

"I'm Castin." I removed my hat with a subtle nod before placing it back on. "I know you're Theia." Her braids partially concealed her face, but I recognized her without a doubt.

"How?" she asked quietly, her eyes wide with shock.

"Let's just say that I've heard a few people mention you. Do you know what just happened in the armory?"

She shook her head a bit too eagerly. "Not at all."

"Smoke was suspiciously seen around that Zekiel guy's hands after he put on an armor set and fell over."

"I'm not surprised," she whispered, trembling.

She's slipping up. "Why?" I pressed. *Tell me all of your secrets.*

"N-nothing. I only said that because there seems to be a lot out of the ordinary happening here often."

Theia avoided looking at my face, instead focusing on my tattoos. It was as if she already knew how to interpret them, knowing what direction to look in next to follow their coordination. *She recognizes these, doesn't she?* I couldn't help but wonder where exactly I had seen her before.

Her attention locked onto the first tattoo I'd received during my initiation—a depiction of snowy mountains, larger than the rest with two words in tidy cursive just below it:

The Frontier

Wait a second... "Just is interesting, that's all." I told her, noting her attentiveness. *She's from the wanted list of Magic Wielders, one of those representatives from a different planet. The law's going to come after her ruthlessly once she's caught.*

She kept her hands hidden from my view. "What is?"

"That you've practiced *cursed* magic. I know how you got here, and soon everyone else will find out too."

The sun was setting, casting grim dark blue and burnt orange tones across the sky. The wind blew dust specks around, reddening our eyes. I tried not to scratch mine as a tense feeling filled the air. Theia created distance between us and appeared to be dizzy, each step accompanied by faulty footing and a painful wince.

"Are you threatening me?" Theia asked quietly.

I shrugged, my sights fixed on the tattoos she couldn't stop glancing down at. *Never say too much.*

She tried to flip it on me, "How did you get here?"

"I handle toxic chemical cleanup. I agreed to help on a case that was supposed to be quick since, and I quote, 'time has almost run out'. What a joke," I scoffed.

"So, what have you been assigned to do exactly?"

"Apparently screw myself," I grunted. "I was basically tricked into agreeing to this mission. They dropped me off with no explanation of where to find the key. I was only told about the ticking time bomb."

Theia glanced up at the towering warning horn.

"Not up there." I pointed downwards. "It's probably more accurate to refer to it as a magnet, but none of that will matter if we don't find the key in time. That's why I keep a lookout for anyone who is up to no good."

"Everyone knows what you do with the Frontier?" she asked, her tone a mixture of curiosity and accusation.

"I'd say so." I said with a hint of sarcasm, motioning around us, "How is that question relevant?"

"Do they know that *you've* practiced magic?"

The reminder made me tense. *They can't ever know. I need to draw attention to her instead.* "Excuse me?"

I could've sworn that I saw a faint light flickering beneath her left arm, seeming to turn on and off with each uneven breath she took. *Is she activating some sort of command? What was it that she did? It had to do with relocating, not time traveling, but shifting from place to place. I recall that she was able to move people from other planets and then back to Earth. Yes, now I remember... That's it! Theia has the teleportation spell!*

"I'll tell them that you have done similar things. I may not know you well yet... but I know what your tattoos represent. You aren't who you say you are. In fact, most of what you've said to me is hypocritical."

The air was growing thicker with heat as the sun dipped lower. I knew that as night fell, things would only get more tense.

"Go ahead and tell your lie that I'm a Magic Wielder. I'll make sure they find out who you really are first." I kept the rest of my thoughts to myself. *Who do you think they're going to believe?*

An hour later, the atmosphere was indeed tense as most of the citygoers gathered to vote on Theia's fate. The reports I had provided about her secretive practices fueled the discussion, and the shop owners, who had taken it upon themselves to interrogate her, were growing increasingly uneasy with her vague responses. It wasn't just about getting to everyone else before her, but longstanding reputation and loyalty from those in gray played a significant role in tipping the scales in my favor. When word spread about Theia's cryptic past, the consensus to imprison her became almost inevitable.

I learned that Theia had been sent to Salt Crest City by some of our Frontier's upper detectives with the hope that she would help those who had become 'stranded' here. At least, that's what I had read. Most of the records from Crow Library were unreliable, their texts often tampered with. Instead, I had meticulously documented my own experiences, knowing that one day my journals might be disseminated by others. Having administrative access to staff records was a privilege I valued greatly. It allowed me to uncover the troubled history between Theia and another citygoer, Elijah, who once went by the name 'Cloudburst'. Their shared past was marred by criminal wrongdoings and several illegal activities.

He was the first to arrive at the sentencing, which was taking place at the gate's fourth section. The crowd that had gathered outside was restless and growing more uncomfortable by the minute. Elijah's grip on his sword's handle was tight, and his stare never wavered from Theia, who stood alongside Tule and a few others in purple suits. These individuals were tasked with carrying out the indefinite punishments.

Tule's final decision had been influenced by the intense debate that had taken place. The murmurs among the crowd were filled with discontent about the 'senselessness of those who use magic' and how they would 'only get us in more danger'. The atmosphere was thick with apprehension as the citygoers prepared to make their final decision.

Elijah remained silent amidst their comments, his stance displaying no emotion as he observed the proceedings. Tule and Theia were the focal points of attention, standing closest to the crowd, while Zekiel, positioned at the center of the gathering, appeared lost in thought. *Does he know her or something?* We were asked to vote on whether Theia should be allowed to move around freely, be sent to the cell block, or if we wanted to abstain from voting. *I wonder if Zekiel's really wearing the rare item? We'll find out soon enough. I'll check the vaults while my supervisors are distracted. Secrets won't stay buried for long.*

Back and forth, most Salt Crest City inhabitants shared their negative views of 'Magic Wielders'. Their disdain was palpable, and their assumptions were cemented by anyone who had direct dealings with what was perceived as an untouchable realm. The murmurs grew louder as frustration mounted.

Tule's voice cut through the noise as she addressed Elijah directly. "What do *you* think, Elijah?"

He flinched slightly but remained otherwise silent, his expression unreadable. Theia's head turned sharply towards him, taken aback presumably by the revelation of his real name.

The crowd's impatience grew. "Is she able to bring us back?" one person asked, their voice tinged with desperation.

"Lift your finger!" another shouted.

Theia spoke softly, her voice barely audible over the rising din. "It may go wrong. I need to practice before I attempt to. The magic I've harnessed may work in ways that we have no understanding of."

"Just lift it already!" someone demanded.

Tule, trying to restore some semblance of order, waved her hands filled with sheets of paper. Several of them slipped from her grip and fluttered to the ground.

"Everyone, let us please take a vote. If you want Theia to be held captive until a teleportation spell is cast, raise your hand."

Elijah's hand remained lowered, one of the few not raised. Despite his apparent support for Theia, the vote was overwhelmingly against her. The decision was made swiftly: Theia was to be imprisoned in the cell block, where she didn't speak to anyone... for a little while.

Later on, I made my way past the cell block while the commotion surrounding Theia had created the perfect cover for my covert mission. The guards were preoccupied with the possibility of her escape, their vigilance worried about her rather than on any potential breaches in security. *They'd never suspect an insider to get a hold of it.*

The armor I sought was highly coveted, its power noted in the diary entries of my colleagues. It was said to be locked away and well-protected, but with the guards' attention diverted, I saw a rare opportunity.

Spreading panic about Theia to create chaos was a great call at first. I had caused *just* enough commotion to avoid any suspicion while I searched for the invaluable armor that everyone else had overlooked. Many of the Emergency Biohazard guards assumed that Theia would try to escape and make a run from serving her sentence. They were completely on edge, constantly peering over their shoulders, and wandering back and forth from their usual outposts to be closer to where she was.

Navigating through the alleyways, I kept my pace brisk and my attention up ahead. *I'll be there in no time.* The sun had ventured below the horizon, leaving a starless sky showering my path with warm hues. As I rounded a corner, I spotted Elijah engaged in a heated argument with another citygoer in the alley across from me. Their exchange was laden with animosity. *They must be arguing about what happened earlier.*

"So why did you even vote for her to walk freely anyway?" the other man spat distastefully, quite angered. "She's lucky she didn't get banished to the mud for her past."

Elijah's back was turned toward me, but I could hear his defensive tone as I walked by as quickly as possible. "There's more to her than you'll ever know."

"A Magic Wielder? We don't take kindly to those types. They threaten our chances of survival. They're the ones who made this place a wasteland. In fact, I've heard that the creatures are lab experiments gone wrong. They try to hide their secrets far off the grid with no internet access. No one will find us out here."

"So, what is it that you are suggesting then?" he asked, his tone laced with skepticism.

"Everyone should be training to survive the wasteland instead of running in circles around the core worrying about hypothetical spells, potions, and other disinformation," came the stranger's retort.

Elijah almost turned around to see if someone was behind him. I took advantage of the distraction, casting a quick spell through my fingertips to conceal myself. Moving swiftly and silently, I slipped past them, the murmur of their conversation fading.

Just before I rounded the corner, I caught Elijah's voice, now more distant but still urgent. "What if magic is the only thing that will save us?" he challenged, his words hanging in the air.

The question lingered in my mind as I made my way to the secluded workbench. The city's oppressive heat seemed to intensify with every step, pressing down on me as I hurried along. When I finally reached the area, I glanced around to ensure no one was watching. I lifted my hat to wipe the sweat from my brow. *Can't wait to get out of this blistering cesspool of a city. I'm almost one step closer to reuniting with my crew.*

The workbench was covered in faded stickers, exactly as described in the Frontier's records. The time I'd spent deciphering notes had paid off. After rummaging through drawers filled with unusual substances and sharp items, I found what I hoped for.

Here it is! I knew I'd get to this before anyone else.

I quickly utilized the space inside my living quarters to put on the new attire and test its effects. Unfortunately, it didn't do what I needed it to, and I knew that if what I'd researched was right, I'd have to convince another conjurer of magic to use it properly.

Securing it back into the package—wrapped tightly with a yellow caution label—I dressed in my usual attire and headed back to the cell block with a sense of disappointment. I held onto the pack as I stepped outside. *I have to talk to Theia about this. I really need her help.*

"Hey!" A comrade of mine called out as he passed by on his way off shift. "What are you doing with that? It looks like a confidential item. Do you have supervisor access?"

"I was just making sure everything got locked up," I said, trying to sound casual. *Shoot! Should've freed a hand to get an invisible hold before he spotted me! Can't ever get too comfortable!* "I stumbled upon this and was actually on my way to turn it in at the weapon store. That merchant never sleeps." My nervous chuckle and poor attempt at dishonesty did nothing to diffuse the situation.

His expression grew perplexed as he noted my apparent paranoia. "Where did you find this item exactly?"

"Came across it near the nasty trash bins outside Crow Library," I explained, "I'm armed in case anything goes sideways while dropping it off to be appropriately secured."

He raised an eyebrow. "Of course you're armed. Biohazard personnel are always commanded to be. Why would I assume otherwise?"

He knows I'm being untruthful! I have to go! A sour feeling gripped my gut. *He's going to tell my supervisor!* I bolted the opposite way, past storage units, toward the cells.

Tule was working extra hours at the front desk again. Like me, she never seemed to know when to call it a night and go get some proper rest. I had to mosey past her to go down the stairs and speak with Theia, hoping she wouldn't question my motives or plans for the coming hours. A thickly annotated journal, empty coffee mugs, and fallen ash from many smoked joints were scattered across the desk in front of her. She was writing when she sleepily noticed me.

"Wait, Castin," Tule said, waving me over. "I want to speak with you! Can you please stay for a minute?"

I wonder if she has even seen the sun since holding herself down here after the sentencing? It seemed like she hadn't slept or done anything other than work in days. Stacks of paper filled her hands as she motioned for me to come closer.

"You know about the green mist, right?" Tule asked, her voice strained with urgency. "You should review what I have here. Please give it a quick read."

I looked over the notes that appeared to be written hastily, with misspelled words scratched out:

B-EYE 345 GREEN MIST

It is said that the cure can be found in nature. There is a hint within the ~~numrical~~ numerical sequence 429, in a small white box, black text. For some reason, it has ~~signficance~~ significance. The answer is tied to these digits! Its medicinal properties can be ~~usd~~ used topically or internally, there is litt-

I stopped reading as I noticed more coffee-stained paragraphs underneath. "You really think I wanna stand here and read a book right now?" I said, impatience creeping into my voice. "I don't have these weapons holstered on me for show. There's work to be done."

"I know that a lot is at stake," Tule said, setting down everything in her hands and standing up to give me her full attention, "but I also know a few things about you. Even if you don't want me to." She gave me a curious look. "Maybe you'll have some new insight on the chemical compounds that I've been reading about? They sound useful, but also a bit familiar, almost like I've heard some of the Emergency Biohazard crew mention them before."

"I don't want to deal with this right now," I replied tersely, "There's a lot of time-sensitive stuff going on with the law. I have certain... matters I must attend that don't involve you." I carefully kept the package behind my back hidden.

"I thought you'd be willing to help or at least offer some advice on how to fight off the hazardous and supernatural effects," Tule said, looking down at her notes with a small sigh of defeat. "It's surprising that this is your response after all the magic you've faced."

The room was getting hotter by the second, and my annoyance was mounting as I felt time slipping away. *Things might get a whole lot worse for me if I don't keep it moving.* Tule grabbed a brittle hair tie and tried to pull her big, fluffy curls into a bun. The band snapped against the back of her hand, and she flinched at the sharp sting. Shaking off the pain, she gave me a half-hearted smile.

"This heat really sucks, doesn't it?" I broke the silence as we stood across from one another. I doubted that Tule could see my investigative glances around the room, thanks to my giant gray hat covering most of my face. "It's been just as hot since we first met here. Back then, I thought it would at least grow colder over time." I grimaced. *I can't believe she almost saw me using Forced Evolutionary Magic.*

"Look, I'm just saying that you might be helpful. Don't dismiss it just because you don't understand it," she shared her assumption with blunt confidence.

"What makes you think I don't 'understand' magic?" I asked, a hint of defensiveness in my voice.

"I-I meant to say because you don't believe in it," she stammered.

She couldn't have been more wrong. I briefly recalled some of the most exhilarating moments of my life, the secret endeavors I'd undertaken away from prying eyes. Tule had accidentally seen too much back then... but that was alright. I knew better than to admit the truth. Denial was the true key to freedom. *No point in us getting stuck in a longer conversation again.* Wordlessly, I turned and left.

Theia's cell was easy to spot as she was one of the few incarcerated citygoers. The others there had been quickly caught and reprimanded by my crew after being spotted behind the library, engaging in shady dealings with spells and weapons. They were modifying them at a novice level, illegally tampering with Cyorio Arms property they had stolen before being moved to vault storage.

Specks of lava from their failed attempts had been their undoing. *Got to be stealthier than that,* I had thought to myself when I'd investigated what they'd left.

They already had targets on their back from the higher-ups due to their suspicious dark attire and refusal to align with us or those in purple. As I passed by their familiar faces, they threw rocks at the walls behind bars. *Their honest choice of clothing made their allegiance clear—a rookie mistake. They should have pretended to care about the Frontier, like me.*

Theia watched me come down the cement steps to seek her, eyeing the package I kept hidden behind my back. I crouched near the bars of her cell and spoke in a low voice, just loud enough for her to hear. On the edge of her bed, she appeared to be anxiously examining the lines of her fingertips, her sweat-streaked face showing signs of distress.

"We don't have much time to talk, so listen closely," I said, "Trust me on this, *I'm* the one you want to help."

She shoved both hands into her pockets and replied softly, "Castin? Why do you want to speak with me?"

"I've learned more about secrets and certain helpful things from the higher realm you were involved in," I started.

"And what did you find out?" she asked timidly.

"That you are the only planetary fighter who's been able to utilize teleportation so far. I need you to do it again—to send people away to safety. I'm not sure if more will be brought here soon. I don't know of any other way to save their lives. To save us in time."

She crossed her arms with evident discomfort. "You got me behind these bars."

"Yeah, sorry about that, but I'll end up here too if we don't work together now. I know I've put you in a difficult place, but I don't have a lot of time to explain." I took off my hat and ran a shaky hand through my sweaty hair. "Helping me would be in both of our favors. I know you have no reason to trust me, but you should."

"Why? Please give me at least one good reason," she demanded.

"My plan has already backfired," I said, my voice low, "My past with magic is now also being looked into. Just like that, raising any sort of suspicion has opened up issues. I might be up for trial too because of my experiences with the higher realm." I pointed to my forearm tattoos. "You know what these represent, don't you?"

She nodded, taking them in once more.

"Then that means you already know about the Frontier, right? The detectives and the representati—"

Theia cut me off, finally looking up somberly. "Only some of it." Her eyes were starting to water.

"It's all connected," I continued. "The warnings, well, turns out they weren't tall tales. We'll all die very soon if we don't act fast. Those like us—Magic Wielders. We have to be real with each other now. I didn't want to tell you before, but I have no choice. We're on an extraordinary hunt for legendary armor—an item capable of granting the wearer what would normally be uniquely unattainable powers."

"I wasn't sure if you'd admit the truth. Thanks." A single tear fell as she blinked. "Are you sure about all of this? I'm not familiar with this set you mention. Do you have an idea where it could be?"

I finally revealed to her what I was holding. "Absolutely. I thought that poser Zekiel had already gotten to it with that theatrical display at the armory, but he didn't. It might be this one. I tried it out myself, but it didn't grant me what I needed. You should try."

"I'm not sure about this. I can't get hurt again," she said, her voice trembling.

'Hurt'? What is she talking about? "Theia, please. There's no use in being upset about anything right now, especially not the past. We have a chance to turn everything around if we can figure this out."

She took a few steps backward, hiding her tears as they continued to fall. "Let me think it over, please."

The darkness concealed most of her from view. I let out a loud sigh and turned around to give her a few moments of space. When I stopped, my eyes stared blankly up ahead, and Elijah's question echoed in my mind once more. *Maybe his words can convince her?*

"Theia," I called out, returning to the cell door with my hat in hand. I gave her the most convincing tone I could muster despite my stress and hidden doubt. "What if magic is the only thing that can save us?"

Her voice trembled slightly, and she wouldn't look away from me. "I heard someone else say that outside the window."

"Oh, really?" I suppressed a chuckle. "Must be an important coincidence. Maybe it's the truth."

Theia stepped out of the shadows, coming closer than she ever had before. The only thing stopping our noses and lips from touching was the solid, cold metal between us. "I've also been told before that there are no such things as coincidences."

Thank you to whoever that was! Now, let's go! My supervisors may be interrogating me in no time! "Sounds about right. Just try this on. That's all I'm asking."

She finally agreed with a silent nod. I slipped the package underneath the door where there was a gap just wide enough to fit it. I stepped away to the other side of the room, giving her privacy while she changed into the gear. I knew she'd be attempting to use her otherworldly capabilities, so I tried not to make her feel pressured.

Several minutes passed with no response.

"How is it going?" I eventually asked while keeping my head turned away from her cell.

"I'm going to need more time. Please," she said, her voice strained as if she was fighting off an outpour of tears. "We can talk again later."

"What about the armor? I need to know if it will work, if you will be able to cast a teleportation spell."

"Trust *me* now, okay? If I'm able to... you'll know."

TULE

Evening

CHAPTER THREE: SIDE MISSION

WORKING FOR THE FRONTIER HAD BEEN MY first choice when I had to choose a career path. They were responsible for creating and enforcing boundaries across several states under the strict and closely monitored supervision of numerous public relations managers. The Frontier had branched out from an accountability office tasked with not only placing physical barriers, but also concealing confidential records under various laws.

As a recent college graduate, I had looked forward to starting my career, especially when an influx of missions had led me to a beach on a southeastern shore. When I had first arrived to scout the area out, it had been abuzz with an art festival. What would normally have been a deserted ghost town had been transformed with colorful lights, cheerful people, and live performers playing music with tin cans at their feet, collecting tips.

"What's the story behind this place?" I had asked, waiting for a direct answer from the others in my team in Experiment Sciences. We had walked out of sight and hearing range from the event attendees.

"Salt chemicals from a mine ended up in the sea. What used to be a popular lake was eventually destroyed here. That was a long time ago, though, and more's been discovered since then. Please remember that all matters we discuss are confidential," one of them had told me, likely sharing only part of the truth.

"I know we can't discuss these matters publicly," I had said, looking around cautiously.

"Then you can't tell anyone about what's going to happen next," he had warned, his voice low and tense.

Suddenly, the man in front of me had violently shoved one of our coworkers into a wide mud pit. His screams for help echoed as he had fallen deeper, with nothing for him to grab onto.

I gasped out in horror. "Why would you do that?"

"The same will be done to you if you tell anyone."

And that's how I became one of the few who knew about the true origins of Salt Crest City. Because on that day, amidst a peaceful biennale, the Frontier took complete control of the entire area with the use of magic.

Forced Evolutionary Magic.

The tourist attraction, once a familiar place of bittersweet refuge, had been overtaken and doused in dangerous chemicals. Helicopters had filled the sky, and the partying crowd was bewildered. A coworker quickly handed me a camouflage helmet that allowed me to breathe. Green smoke filled most of the sky, and the waters were bubbling.

From that day onwards, bound to work for the Frontier despite my attempts to leave, I believed I had to keep it a secret. That the last thing I could ever do was become a whistleblower, but that only fueled my desire to become one even more—to use my love for reading and speaking to share words with others for the greater good.

Then I met Zekiel.

A mysterious man who turned out to also have a past entwined with magic. Of all the things I found interesting about him, his genuine care stood out the most. I admired how he often got deep in thought; even though he seemed reluctant to discuss matters initially, I knew he would at least ponder it afterward.

One quiet evening, I was excited to enlist his help in creating a diversion at the least busy shop we had—Sea Bartering. With valuable hours already lost, I moved quickly to give the others time to process my warnings. Earlier that day, I had taken audio recordings of passages from the library's catalog about elemental magic; revealing important phrases, unborn prophecies, and warning signals that nature was trying to send us to prepare for a seemingly unbeatable storm.

Not enough people are taking these warnings seriously. My worry grew. *We're already almost out of time. Those on my side will run out of patience soon.*

I recorded everything in two hours, sharing what I thought was key information. "There are only fifty hours remaining," I declared. "We are running out of time. A storm will be upon us soon, and many will get sick. We have to act fast. There are only fifty hours left."

The tapes, each running for a total of six minutes, were tucked away in my shoulder bag. I entered the Sea Bartering shop, and the small bell above the door rang. The clerk straightened up behind the counter, watching us suspiciously as Zekiel followed closely. He checked that his antique register was locked. The store was filled with hidden treasures—rusty signs for sale, torn-up chairs covered in paint splatter, and a vintage drive-in sign.

There were also several unfamiliar items tucked away in the dimly lit dust. A few of them had been covered in graffiti of tired faces and various phrases with profanity.

"Lemme know if you need anything," the merchant spoke in a groggy voice. The majority of his face was covered by a big fisher's hat that he never took off. A patch of netting hung over his wary expression.

"We're just looking around," I replied, careful not to reveal what we were really planning to do. I needed to catch him off guard long enough for the message to be shared, even if only for just a few moments.

"*Yeah*. Sure thing. I'm here if you have questions," he said, studying us with a cautious eye.

I turned to Zekiel. "What do you think of all this?"

He caught sight of his reflection in one of the broken mirrors. "Looks like it's been through a lot." Then he touched some dry seashells strung together to make a wind chime, setting off a domino effect as they swayed and clinked against one another.

Nearby was a small pantry section with shelves upon shelves of bread loaves rolled in paper. Next to them were rusty, noisy old fridges filled with butter.

"Are you hungry?" I asked.

"Starving." Zekiel raised his voice so the merchant could hear him, "Have anything else to eat?"

"Did you not see the signs?" he grumbled. "No."

I grabbed a few slices of bread and used a broken knife to spread the only topping available on them. I handed him a piece of toast and he ate it quickly.

"Wow, this is… *really* salty," he remarked, grimacing slightly.

"You're going to have to pay for that, Tule," the merchant warned, crossing his arms.

"I know."

"Just making sure you don't think you have special privileges. I couldn't care less who you're associated with," he added, his voice sharp.

Zekiel spoke quietly, "Let's go where he can't watch us."

We took our food—slices of bread slathered in butter—to the back of the store and admired some of the artwork while eating. Zekiel neared one of the signs that was smaller than the others.

PLEASE SAVE US

"What really happened here?" He touched the painted cry for help. "Who made it into what it is?"

"Salt Crest City wasn't always like this. It even had a different name back then." I wasn't sure how much to say.

"How long ago?" Zekiel asked.

"The nineteen-hundreds," I replied, glancing at him.

"Well, I mean, I'd *expect* it to change over time."

"No. It became a ghost town; not due to passing time, but because of ecological disaster and… work-related conflict. We were stationed here due to how isolated and desolate the land was," I explained, my voice quiet.

"What sort of 'ecological disas—"

The merchant interrupted our conversation. "This isn't a place to dine and chat."

That couldn't have been timed any better. I wasn't ready to share much about the city's history yet. I was more concerned with the present events and the timer that was ticking in the back of my mind. *Hours are getting scarcer,* I reminded myself as I caught sight of a ladder out of the corner of my eye. I leaned closer to Zekiel and whispered, "That leads to the upper story. Can you please distract him for a minute while I plant the tapes?"

Zekiel nodded, though his eyes shone with concern. "Of course. Please be careful while on those planks, though."

I glanced up and noticed how several were falling apart. Jagged pieces of wood, once part of a solid deck, were seconds away from caving in on themselves.

"Thank you for the warning."

Zekiel went to the survivor manning the front, and I listened to their voices as I sneaked away quietly.

"Need something?" he asked begrudgingly.

"Do you have anything to read about this place?" Zekiel replied, trying to keep the shop owner's attention.

"You serious? Everything from the past is outdated, including that library. Make sure you don't get caught up with those who have their heads in the clouds," the merchant grouchily spread misinformation.

"So, there were brochures?" he inquired.

"Yeah. This place used to be some sort of a tourist spot or something. None of that matters now, though. What else can I help you with?"

"Why don't you tell me about the sea dragon?" Zekiel promptly suggested.

The other man sighed. "You know about the leviathan, yet I don't see one wield-worthy weapon on you. You're bold, but perhaps not as gifted as a few have claimed you to be."

"Who called me 'gifted'?" Zekiel refrained from looking up at me as I made it to the next level and tiptoed above them towards the sound system.

"The Magic Wielder who got sent to the cell."

There were a few seconds of uncomfortable silence before he changed the topic, "What do you suggest I carry?"

"How about a pistol? There are some decent deals and starter choices, especially for someone who probably can't afford any nicer ones. Though you will have to pay in *our* currency." He leaned down behind the counter and pulled out a square metal box, setting it down with a heavy thud. "Why don't you see for yourself? There are thousands of screws in here."

The lid squeaked as he opened it. "How are these valuable?"

I took a tape out of my pocket and loaded it into the player. As I turned up the volume, I watched the two below me, stealing glances through the gaps in the floorboards.

"Look around." The merchant pointed at the items near him and even to Zekiel's armor. "Weapon and armor modifications. Restoring decorative pieces. Making equipment. Trying to cling to some sense of normalcy. You name it. They're needed, and they sell, so that's what we use. They are also hard to come by here. I have what would be considered a small fortune."

Zekiel picked up a large screw. "So, this..."

"Is the equivalent of twenty-five bay dollars," the man replied.

"Alright then. How can I get some?"

"See who needs help around here. Accept any small quests you can take. You'll be rewarded based on how well you do," the merchant advised, his voice gruff.

Static crackled in the shop's speakers for a few seconds, and my heart raced. Then, I heard my voice repeating loudly in the playback, "Time is running out. We will die if we don't discover the key to survival. The green cracks are coming. We may lose many lives. We have to find the answer in nature. The sequence four, two, nine is valuable because—"

"Turn that garbage off!" the shop owner yelled as I climbed down from the second story. "Why are you meddling with our equipment? Leave it alone!"

Zekiel jumped in without hesitation to my defense, "The word has to get out. Just let her play this, please."

"They are fairy tales that only perpetuate panic!" the dealer shot back angrily with his arms up.

I glanced out of the foggy window to see that almost all of the citygoers outside had stopped what they were doing to listen to my recording. Castin, who was easy to spot in the crowd because of his sizable gray hat, seemed the most caught off guard as he stood mysteriously in an alleyway across from the Loot Vaults.

Zekiel and I were kicked out of the store and informed that we wouldn't be allowed back inside for a while. We shrugged off the owner's angry words and calmly left. My message only played for a short while after that until it came to a screeching halt, a different recording taking its place. Rich, drawn-out notes of a well-tuned guitar began to play, and I closed my eyes momentarily, letting the mellow song wash over me.

"What do you think about what happened earlier?" I asked over the music. "You know, with Theia? Not sure if you could tell, but I was nervous up there."

"Why? You weren't the one on trial," Zekiel responded, his brow furrowing.

"I know, but carrying out those commands, answering to someone else that outranks me... What I have to do can get really difficult sometimes." I sighed.

"It will all blow over soon... the commotion around magic. Before you know it, there will be someone, or something, new that everyone will get concerned about. It's only a matter of time," he reassured me.

"I'm not so sure about that. What we just shared will bring even more panic and divide."

"Well, sooner or later, the events will unfold. How will people deny the truth when it's right before them?"

"It will be too late." I shook my head. "Zekiel... Do you think it was wrong to put Theia behind bars?"

"Everyone came to a vote fairly."

"*Was* it fair, though? She's caused no trouble since arriving. Sure, she hasn't helped save us, but maybe she would've come around if she wasn't already punished for the past." I nodded to one of his hands as we stood outside of the store. "Speaking of which... have you seen it again? The smoke from your palms?"

"No. I'm not sure what that was all about, anyway." He pulled his hand from view shyly and then put both in each leather pocket. "Probably meant nothing."

"Maybe it was a sign about your armor. That may have been a clue! What if the key we're looking for is inside a set? Perhaps wearing a specific piece will give us the power we need—like yours?"

Zekiel looked at the ground doubtfully. "Maybe."

"We should stop by the weapon's workbench to look through the storage units. It's not far from here, and some things are more valuable than those sold in the shop. Maybe the key has been right in front of us the whole time. Something so invaluable, yet it wasn't even given a price tag?" I suggested.

"You really think the key to safety is sitting in a pile of free items?" Zekiel replied, skeptical.

"Just because something's free doesn't mean it has no value. People overlook hidden treasures all the time here. That's why I make it a point to collect and display them. It's worth a shot to see if it's there. Let's head over quickly before anyone else gets the same idea."

ELIJAH

Evening-Night

48 hours remaining
CHAPTER FOUR: TAPE RECORDINGS
I HAD STARTED TO FEEL LIKE THE CHOSEN

one. I had a lot of experience with facing challenging times and overcoming infinite obstacles. Survival had always been the most important thing to me, especially when I was overburdened by life's unfair punishments. It was as if those who did the right things were penalized, but those who advocated for evil were rewarded. People had grown too desperate for power.

This isn't right... was the thought that echoed in my mind as I watched Theia receive her sentence. She and I had been through a lot together. We'd met in the most surreal way—in front of a tall blue castle floating high up in a cloudy sky. I had gone from taking a much-needed nap on the beach of my hometown, Asperhill, to opening my eyes and finding an unknown woman standing before me.

Theia, just as bewildered as I was, wondered how we could be so closely connected despite being complete strangers. She claimed to have 'manifested' me onto a planet designed to explore consciousness, and as a representative of one of its factions, she had carried out spells and commands for whatever influence she was under.

At first, I had demanded to be set free. I fought as hard as I could against the three leaders who had quickly forced me into doing a long list of terrible tasks. Yet after becoming Theia's right-hand man, I got to know her on a deeper level than anyone else. It was not just because of her intimate ability to read my thoughts and speak to me through them, but also her ability to feel, care, and have a sensitivity toward the lives of others.

A part of me still yearned for closure about what happened on that planet before she freed me. The conversations and plans we had, the cryptic remarks she made—they all remained within my subconscious. Despite not getting many answers, I did the best I could to make peace with the fact that I'd probably never see her again. *Maybe that's what's best. I need to move on; at least we're no longer in contact.*

Or so I thought...

Back in the small town of Asperhill, I worked hard to reintegrate into my routine, which typically led to me visiting one of the many nearby beaches. I decided to drive farther than usual, to a southeastern shore about three hours away from my home.

I had a lot on my mind, but all the songs on my go-to playlist did nothing but remind me of everything I was trying to forget. The highway was nearly empty as I drove through the misty rain to my destination. *Swimming will help with these hot flashes.*

Other visitors gave me odd looks for bringing one of my swords along at my side. It was from an important part of my past, passed down from a friend, and I kept it as a reminder of humanity and survival—to not lose one in pursuit of the other. I walked along the shore alone, which was initially relaxing, but then reality set in, and history began to repeat itself.

A portal appeared near the ocean cliffs, and Tule stepped through, asking for help to save people in a time-sensitive mission. I stood in shock and awe as she suddenly appeared before me, looking scared and desperate. I took a few cautious steps back to create some much-needed distance. I had no idea who she was as the portal revealed the bleak, flat, endless mudscape. It wasn't the first time that I'd been approached by a stranger through a warped sense of reality and presented with a new challenge to survive.

The warm, humid air from her side intermingled with the ocean breeze where I stood. The land around her stretched for miles, nearly empty. I could tell she was off the grid, far from the rest of civilization.

"It's a long shot for me to ask, but I need you to come with me!" she pleaded.

"I don't know you! What could you possibly need from me?"

"Your help! The... realm has gotten out of hand!" She pointed towards what looked like a city beyond the portal.

My sights drifted to the twelve ominous buildings, and a chill washed over me, as cold as the waves I'd just been swimming in. "I'm not sure what you're even asking!"

A worried half-smile appeared on her face. "But you're sure of who Theia is."

Just like that, my attention was captured. "Y—why?"

"She needs your assistance!" Tule urged as the gateway began to close.

"What?" I took a few frantic steps towards her.

She motioned for me to follow. "You have to act fast!"

I quickly stepped into a futuristic yet dystopian space and took in a deep breath of the hot air. A stinging heat hit my skin as I watched the portal close behind us. Tule led me through the city, stressing the importance of what was happening. She also mentioned how useful my sword would be.

Despite my last-second decision to help, I quickly found myself unsure of how to approach the situation at hand. I had hardly been able to focus on the new sights, survivors, or discoveries around me as Tule showed me where everything was located.

Ever since I last saw Theia at Asperhill's chilling falls, I struggled to fully understand our past memories. She was the one who occupied a piece of my mind that I never consented to give. I was routinely made to weather the storms of life with a brave face, but my desire for closure was never truly fulfilled. *So much time was stolen.* It had been a long while since we last spoke. Even though she told me she couldn't hear my thoughts anymore, I didn't believe her. *She may always have a part of my mind.*

The parting words I gave her—*Move on from the past*—turned out to be advice I needed to heed myself. I knew that she wasn't an evil person, that she had hit rock bottom, and her actions were not that of a sober mind. Yet even though I felt a connection to her, I knew deep down that our ties were forever tarnished. No future for us could involve peace.

I had become exhausted from constantly monitoring my thoughts in an unnatural way, experiencing such an insurmountable lack of privacy and yearning for proof of my complete freedom. I needed to be sure that there were no ties still lingering between us.

But how can I know for sure that I truly am free?

What made the most sense at the time was to make Theia believe that some part of me desired to be with her. A distorted truth, as part of me was only enamored by the unique gifts she could grant me.

I have nothing left to say to her. I mean, where do I even begin to confront my captor? What she has done is her burden, not mine. I don't want our lives intertwined ever again, yet it seems we might have to work together once more. How will I ever find closure? Does it even exist?

Tule gave me a rundown of the buildings and groups but kept us on a fast track to the residential quarters. It was in the claustrophobic hallways that she tried to convince me to knock on Theia's door within the first twenty minutes of arriving. She had anticipated her plan to work faster than she thought it would, but I had to break the bad news.

"I'm not ready yet." The black leather armor I had been told to promptly change into made my hot anxiety flashes ten times more unbearable. "Sorry."

She walked back from Theia's living space, making her way towards me as I trailed behind at a distance. "What do you mean? You *just* chose to come here. I don't want to pressure you, okay? But your help is needed."

"I know I agreed to this, but what matters more is how you even found me and why you chose to speak with me. We can get into that later." I looked down at the books she was carrying. *Could've sworn I've seen a few of these before. Are they what I think they are? How?*

"But now that I'm here, I just need a few more minutes before I see her again. Face to face, in person, that is."

"Alright… but I urge you to figure out what you want to say quickly. Time is of the essence. She's refused to speak to others here so far, which is *probably* for the best, but things could get out of hand."

She's really here. I can't even believe it. I kept my distance from Theia as I sorted out my thoughts. *What if this goes wrong? What if she gets hurt again by being involved in these powers? There must be another way besides risking her life. If she sees me, hears my name, she just might. I'll find another way out instead.*

During my fleeting downtime, I established a handful of friendships with the merchants who occasionally gave me free items or offered small quests in exchange for what they called 'bay dollars'. *I want to be on their good side in case things take a turn for the worse.* For the most part, I kept my head down and was cautious of trusting those I had just met.

Eventually, the only buildings I hadn't explored were the Loot Vaults. Regardless of where I stood, the gigantic metal structure loomed over us all. *I need to find out what's in those.* Given the strict security around the area, I had a better chance of discovering more at the public library.

That evening, I visited the location, which turned out to be one of the hottest places. The windows were designed to let only small rays of light in near the ceiling, and there was no way to open or ventilate the space properly. Breathing became significantly more difficult as I stepped inside, and I coughed into my arm. It was then I noticed another man walk down one of the aisles not far from where I stood.

He held a book and wore dark-framed glasses that were in contrast to his bluish eyes. "Are you okay?" His attire was all-black, but instead of leather or metal armor, he wore a vintage coat, pants, and combat boots.

"I'm doing fine, thanks. It's just extremely dusty in here," I replied, observing the specks floating in the dry air.

"Yeah, I'm grateful to not have a dust allergy." He stepped past a few tables to introduce himself.

I glanced at him more closely, and a flicker of recognition sparked in my mind. "I think I've seen you at the Sea Bartering shop?"

"I help where I can. You'll find me here or there."

"I'm Elijah. Nice to meet you," I said, extending my hand.

"You can call me the Librarian," he said with a friendly smile, shaking mine in return. "Likewise."

"How long have you been here?" I asked, curious.

"A few weeks. I've mainly spent my time reading these books," he explained, handing me one. "You might find this interesting. It's a pretty quick read."

The book's corners were sharp, outlined in a gold finish, and the wrappings of painted vines snaked over the edges. I flipped through the pages and noticed a repetitive use of the word 'green' to describe elements and characteristics of weapon types found on the grim ruins of Salt Crest City.

I faced the Librarian. "What can you tell me that's useful to know?"

"It would take a long time to go over. I'm still trying to piece it together, in fact. I'm not sure I can guide you. Perhaps read some of it yourself? This title right here is one of the few that seems to be informative, though, a guide to something," he suggested, pointing to a book on the shelf.

I wonder what secrets are in these? The only thing I enjoyed more than reading was discovering the story behind a book's creation. *What else can I learn about other fighters and the planets they were on?* "Do you mind if I take this manuscript with me?" I asked the Librarian.

"It's all yours. I was just going to put it back on the shelves before it got lost in this sea of paperbacks," he replied.

I thanked him for his time and left the library, the weight of unanswered questions heavy on my mind, making it hard to maintain any small talk. I was already deep into the eighth diary before I even stepped back outside. *What if they have more clues about elemental magic?* I felt a surge of adrenaline rush through me as I tapped my fingers against the hardcover. Just then, I noticed a section for journal entries while scanning the table of contents.

Date: Unknown, Another Wasted & Dreary Day

No idea where we are and what's truly going on. There's no way to escape this heat, and we're all becoming dehydrated. Other people keep arriving on the outskirts where the dragon sleeps. I hear them argue with one another, blaming each other for a problem that no one knows how to solve. Some survivors claimed that they used to have 'magical abilities' too. I wonder what would happen if there was the option to share them?

* -C*

I briefly reflected on my knowledge of armor designed for what were known as 'planetary fighters'. One book, *So On They Went,* outlined the unique makeups and builds of powerful elements unlike any others that granted abilities. A specific armor set, its origins marked as unknown in the description, had the capability of granting the wearer someone else's powers entirely.

Wait... That's it! The armor capable of transfer! It can send us home! It's here, it has to be... This has to be the right place! We just have to put it on and–

I almost dropped the book when I realized I needed to find it before someone else did—someone who wouldn't grasp the chaos it could unleash.

There were no clear rules outlined in this text; all the writings about it were eerily vague. One notable feature, however, was the sea dragon emblem where a clothing tag would typically be. I finally recalled what I had learned about its unique capabilities.

Poetry throughout what I read had given clues to where certain items could be found. Salt Crest City aligned with one of the handwritten poems that I had memorized from prior readings:

> *Where the sky's always dark,*
> *Where dangerous threats lurk below.*
> *A muddy city's hidden riches,*
> *A key concealed between lines.*
> *One sea dragon emblem given life,*
> *One chance to escape poison.*

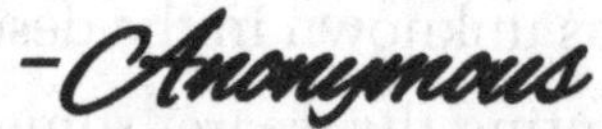

So much could be destroyed if it falls into the wrong hands. I stayed dressed in all black as I set out to search, hoping to avoid drawing attention to myself. I recalled the emblem's description:

THE EMBLEM OF EMBER

Level: Legendary
Use: Acquire Magic
Duration: 30 Seconds
Special: Grants Other Planetary Fighter's Abilities

What if someone else gets Theia's power? I ran to the armory and then to every other shop. Table after table, I searched. The subtle sun gradually sank lower in the sky. I checked every crate, cabinet, and hole in the ground large enough to fit an armor set. I kept a torch lit in my hand to help me see the storage units better. Despite my extensive hunt, I hadn't found it.

The horn let out a chilling sound that sent shivers down my spine. We shook as mud crumbled back into its ocean form, granting the deep's inhabitants room to swim. Moonlight bounced off the dark waters before they were breached. Something rose and rumbled the city's tottering foundation. A tail emerged from the surface, covered in barnacles that secreted virulent green bubbles. The creature swam around the city a few times before disappearing back beneath the contaminated water.

I kept wiping sweat from my forehead as I looked around, despite coming up empty-handed. Desperate,

I then dashed to each wardrobe, rummaging through the clothing, checking tag after tag.

No metal... yet. Someone must already have it.

One drawer screeched open, rusted hardware, protesting loudly enough to ensure anyone from neighboring rooms could hear me looking around where I shouldn't have been. *Don't want to get falsely accused of anything and end up in a cell too. I don't know enough about this Frontier.* I suspected that a skeptical guard was on their way to interrogate me when I heard unfamiliar noises down the hall.

I doused my torch in a bucket of foul, stagnant water in the corner of the room and held my breath while waiting in the darkness. The sounds of doors opening and closing echoed, accompanied by the heavy stomps of someone's boots headed in my direction.

They may not be open to hearing me explain anything. I slowly drew my standard two-handed sword, thankful again for being able to afford it after completing some basic quests for a few other citygoers.

A silhouette of someone with long, disheveled hair appeared in the doorway seconds later. They held a tiny candle that barely illuminated the mostly barren room. From what I could see, they weren't armed with anything substantial—just a combat knife that wouldn't do much damage in our current situation.

"Who's in here?" I recognized Zekiel's voice.

I stepped forward with a sigh of relief so he could see me. "I want to ensure that I'm making use of all magical offerings. The books we have are here for a reason. They have keys—information that…" I took the candle from his hand and led him to the window, wiping the dust away with my sleeve, "lights our paths."

The moonlit ocean shimmered behind the warm flame.

He tapped onto the glass. "The portals we went through to get here were from the same realm, right? So, we're on the same side, regardless of our attire—"

"What 'side' is that? What is it you stand for?" I challenged, surprised at his impactful choice of words.

"Justice. Helping those trying to make progress."

"Really? In doing what?" *What has he gotten done?*

"I'm sure you heard the message playing through the speakers earlier that Tule made. I care for the same thing you were just trying to introduce me to. Magic. Heeding the warnings that have been prophesied," he explained, his tone growing more passionate yet sad.

"What do you know about that?" I asked him, my curiosity piqued.

"Too much. Words spread faster than fire, and magic burns even stronger. All it takes is one weak link for everything to unravel. What do *you* know?"

"Respectfully? More about what's going on than a lot of others," I replied, my voice steady. "People say to keep your enemies close, but I don't agree. Keep those close who have wisdom to share and absorb as much of it as you possibly can."

I can't mention the legendary armor unless absolutely necessary. I've heard he's untrustworthy. I need to tell him something not as important. Well... hopefully it won't be. "I heard the tapes. The green smoke will arrive before we know it. It's said that lightning will crack open the sky like 'glass'. It will eat away at the atmosphere and release a poison that causes debilitating eye infections if left untreated."

Zekiel looked out at the dark clouds. "Do you know what the cure is?"

"No, but the poison leaks for a few minutes."

A rumble of muffled thunder underscored my words, as the night brought forth new terrors from below, beginning to claw their way to the surface. The sounds of their scratching grew even closer, while infected magic wove its way through the crumbling ecosystem.

"With your knowledge of the bunker books..." Zekiel broke the brief silence. "Where did this all originate from? The mud, mutants, and magic?"

"The books didn't say much about the wastelands of Earth, but those that do are apparently found in Crow Library."

"So, you don't know what was here before us?" Zekiel mused. "I may be wrong, but it looks like some sort of theme park. How else would you explain the random fixtures and types of equipment lying around this place?"

"You didn't hear *any* news of what happened back on Earth while you were away, did you?" I asked, watching him carefully.

"No. Why?"

"Let's just say you might want to have a conversation with Tule about her occupation, especially if you're planning to become closer friends with her." I gave him a nod. "Although talking's been nice with you, I have other matters to attend to."

"So do I," Zekiel said, "I'm going to continue helping out the Experiment Sciences crew with placing flyers around. I probably won't get even an hour of sleep tonight." He motioned to the folded stack of papers hidden under one of his arms. "I'm surprised you aren't helping. Unless you wanted to look for Theia on your own?"

"*Wait*. What are you talking about?" My throat burned as a bout of acid reflux hit me with a wave of worry.

"I'm surprised you don't know yet... you must be on a dedicated mission. Theia took one of Tule's keys from her belt when she went down to the cell block. The Frontier has just begun issuing warnings to the entire city and imploring us to spread the word. Everyone's already keeping their weapons closer than ever, and panic about spells is re-emerging."

"Can I see the message that's on those flyers?" My hand shook as I reached out to take one from him.

He handed it to me without asking any questions and watched as I observed it under the dimming light, the candle close to burning out. Someone had drawn a black and white portrait of Theia with a troubling message:

WARNING:

MAGIC MAKER ON THE LOOSE

Theia has escaped! Be careful of her sinister curses!
Reward of 10,000 bay dollars for whoever finds her!

ZEKIEL

Night

CHAPTER FIVE: MEDKIT

ELIJAH IMMEDIATELY LEFT TO FIND THEIA.

I took a moment to enjoy some much-needed silence in the safe room, where a dusty antique typewriter sat on a nearby table. *Facing problems in the coming hours is inevitable.* Peculiar things kept happening, and so many people needed saving. It was mentally exhausting to keep pushing onward despite the stress of potentially letting everyone else down. After arriving with a target already on my back, I felt not only a need to save others but to prove myself.

I couldn't bring back those who had died before. *Jasmine... Saige... Amira...* The list went on, and I thought about each of them every single day. I had to confront and eventually accept the frustrating fact that I would never get to see any of them again or exchange the words I wanted to tell them so badly. The grief felt like it was corroding away at my heart. I feared that one day I would become nothing more than a jaded shell of my former self.

At least I can try my best to help others now. Especially Tule. It's nice to have a friend again. My attention was drawn to a moving light that looked to be near the Sea Bartering shop. *Is that her out there? Who'd be out there right now?* I gripped my combat knife and left the living quarters to go investigate.

The store had already been locked up for the night. A few of the decorative wind chimes outside tapped into each other as they swayed, the sound reminiscent of heavy raindrops hitting the ground.

I felt a pang of nostalgia at the melody, trying to suppress memories of my family's front porch and my mother's voice calling me inside, mingling with the sound of the chimes. I tried to think as little as possible about my past and those I hadn't talked to in years.

I quickly approached the unfamiliar glow, the stranger not far behind as I drew closer. The path was lit by my candle that Elijah had hurriedly given back before he ran off to search for Theia. *A reward of ten thousand bay dollars would help me get a much better weapon.* For the first time in a long while, I felt a bit of wonder. *Maybe I could purchase a sword of my own?*

"Looking to buy something?" a voice called out as the distance between us closed. The man had a black bandana covering half of his face and similarly colored hair swaying at either side of it. He lifted both of his coat flaps to reveal rows of pockets. "Schematics, potions, valuables that are on a *different* type of market. I also have great magical items to make use–"

"I'm not interested in things pertaining to magic," I cut him off while waving my hands dismissively.

"You ended up in the wrong city, then, because this place is filled with it. I also have some potent joints if you'd prefer to purchase those instead? Or writing utensils?" He showed me some of what he mentioned under the moonlight, until he reached the book collection. There was a bag of them near his feet that was spilling over. "These... aren't for sale."

"What I need to buy first is a proper weapon since this is all I have," I said and showed him my knife. "But... yeah I might come back around for a joint or two. Thanks for letting me know. I really need to take the edge off." *I've needed to for a very long while.*

"I agree with you–especially about the first part. That may be good for prying open rusted jars of butter, though I can promise you it won't do much more than that. Trust me, if you know about the things I've read, you'll be as prepared as possible out here." He gave a little tap on something tucked away in his coat.

"Noted." I still had no idea who the masked man was, but I refrained from asking for his name, as he was clearly trying to stay under the radar. *I don't blame him for remaining anonymous. I'll lay low too in a place like this.* "I'm going to go see what I can do about gearing up."

"Sounds like a good idea. I'd personally recommend setting your sights on obtaining one of Euphrasia Arm's katanas. They're quite durable, slender, and their single-edged blades tend to inflict a lot of damage. Maybe this can help you out in purchasing something," he discreetly handed me some screws from his pocket which sounded full of many. "You should add these to whatever else you can earn to get something decent. Weaponry doesn't come cheap here. Hope you have a safe night." With that, he stepped back into the shadows without another word.

"Thank you. I appreciate the help," I said before turning to leave. *I should have asked him about medkits.*

Ever since my arrival, I've had my sights set on one of the swords that had crossed my mind several times. Without one equipped, I felt vulnerable and unable to defend myself against threats I would inevitably face. I recalled again what I'd learned from Tule. *Much worse is on the way, but I'll figure out how to become prepared.*

The weapons store was the only one open both day and night. Neon lights shone over an expansive inventory on each wall's display, and the back of the shop featured a shooting range assembled from lined telephone booths, with each scrap metal target board painted differently. All of them dangled by shredded threads of fishing line bundles.

Most of the surrounding space was filled with a variety of unplugged screens that had been painted, their vibrant colors chipped and faded into a weather-beaten style.

On the main counter, all of the product options were laid out on a singular flimsy packet. Dust flew into the air with each turn of a page. The images inside were accompanied by someone's unsteady handwriting in old, splattered ink. The first page listed swords, the second throwables, the fourth guns, and the fifth detailed maps and schematics of varying sizes and styles.

I took a closer look at the final page of the packet, which displayed a spiderweb-like map of muddy tunnels. They appeared to be a tangled mess, each pathway growing progressively more complicated the further down each level went.

Flipping back to the previous page listing weapons, I noticed that the cost of each wasn't written inside. Instead, every selection stated, 'Ask the shop owner for prices'.

Each weapon was neatly outlined, color-coded, and assigned various magic-level requirements. I wasn't sure what acquiring one entailed, or if I had one at all, but chose to not ask due to keeping my past a secret.

GUNS

Wire	**Timepiece**
Pistol *M.lvl:* 2	SMG *M.lvl:* 7
Train Wreck	**SOS**
Assault Rifle *M.lvl:* 5	Shotgun *M.lvl:* 10

"You gonna order anything?" the dealer asked, breaking my focus.

"Yeah, in a moment. I have a lot on my mind."

"Don't we all?" he replied with a shrug.

I skipped the second page and returned to the swords, where there were many options to choose from.

SWORDS

Pipe Bolt	**Doubles**
1 Handed *M.lvl:* 3	2 Handed *M.lvl:* 8
TDCC	**Wishing Well**
Increased damage upon energy depletion *M.lvl:* 6	Temporarily stun and damage up to lvl 20 *M.lvl:* 12

"Is this still available?" I asked, pointing to a light gray sword branded with a cloud symbol in the middle of it. It looked like a simple, lightweight choice with what I thought was a moderate magic-level requirement. *Let's see if I can get this without a 'level'.*

"No. Some of these have already been claimed by others. You have to get here early when more stock is available, especially before the collectors arrive. They always get one of everything," the merchant explained.

"Really? For what purpose?" Then I briefly thought about Tule and all of the stuff she collected in her already cramped space. *She's definitely one of them. I don't recall seeing that many weapons, though, mostly what others consider junk. I wonder if I can be gifted one?*

"Bringing them joy, I suppose. I don't mind the extra business anyway." The man shrugged again.

I remained silent, unsure of how to respond, and finding it challenging to get my mind off of the conversation I had with Tule over our small drinks. She revealed so much to me soon after my arrival—her paintings and the warnings—but she also alluded to the significant divide when it came to weapon choices.

The strangers' eyes followed each option that was mounted on the walls. "Just as silence conveys a message like words, be careful when choosing what type you wield. You'll be taking more of a stance than you realize." His smile fell once the guns transitioned into swords, then his expression turned into one of distress.

I'd prefer to fight with a sword. Something told me to keep my opinions to myself due to his hostile look.

The bell rang as another man with short platinum blond hair stepped into the shop, his outfit entirely gray and a pensive look in his eyes. He went to browse over the catalog.

"Hey, Ezra. Let me know if you need anything," the merchant said while promptly shoving a stack of what looked to be missing person posters inside a drawer.

The stranger seemed to be on a mission while making his way through the first part of full shelves. "When do I not need something?" he replied while recounting screws and re-reading the news headlines.

"You mean your 'friends'?" the owner grumbled, "By the way, I'm sorry about what happened to your sister. The portal disappearances have been hard to hear about. Everyone's doing all that they can to help."

"I miss Lorelai a lot, but I'm hopeful we'll find her," Ezra said and then gave me a hypervigilant side-eye.

My attention remained on the initial task at hand despite the new visitor and the eerily familiar name he just mentioned. "How much does, uh, this one go for?" I asked, pointing to a steel sword that looked to have the sharpest blade out of every choice along with attention-grabbing elemental properties.

"Nine-hundred and eighty-five bay dollars." He nodded to the other unique ones surrounding it as they also glowed enchantingly in differing tones. "These range from seventy to a couple thousand."

I placed my screws onto the counter. "Well, I have these, which might allow me to get something simple."

The merchant burst into one of the loudest laughs I had ever heard. "Bay dollars aren't *that* simple. One screw only gives a dollar value if it's in a certain condition. Size, rust level, if there are any chips, or if the screw has come into contact with any illegal substances. You still have a lot more to learn."

"Would you be interested in assisting me with a side quest?" Ezra inquired my way once the other man had calmed down again. "I'll reward you with bay dollars that you can put towards buying a sword."

It sounds like it would be a good idea to agree. Maybe I'll spot Theia in the meantime. I'll definitely be able to afford something if I help with the search. I'd rather not go there first, though. "What do you need me to do?"

"Let's talk on the way, alright? We have to get something important for someone close to me. Head with me to the residential rooms to recruit more help."

Puddles of light covered the flooring where the moon shone through damaged wall panels. The hot air left droplets of condensation on the unclean windows and rotting wood. We asked many of the others to assist with the job but were ignored or denied until someone finally decided to join twenty minutes later.

Ezra knocked five times on a silver door, the taps from his knuckles sending echoes down the hall. "Hey, Castin. Something has gotten out of hand on the mud. Can we talk?" He had to wait in silence for a bit, gave me a shrug, and then knocked five more times.

"It's supposed to be six, remember? Also, don't state my name during deals. You never know who else could be listening." I heard Castin's muffled voice on the other side of the door, which was opened to reveal his bunk bed, the bottom occupied with a collection of guns, ammunition, and modification attachments. The desk next to them had a crumpled water bottle resting on it, with less than half left to drink. "Oh. Zekiel. *You're* here. Great. How about a heads-up next time, Ezra?"

"You're running low on water too?" I asked after ignoring the sarcastic greeting. "That's tough."

"Others pour heavy-handedly," he replied, taking a swig. He motioned for us to step inside. "Gotta see what I can get tomorrow from the bartering rations."

We walked inside, and instantly Ezra and Castin started catching up while I glanced at a journal left open on the table. When the other two weren't looking at me I took the opportunity to see what the entry read:

Date: Unknown, Screwed-Up Night

Growing impatient with this heat. We're nearly suffocating. Feel like I've woken out of a drunken stupor. Up earlier than everyone else. When looking out of this sad excuse for a window, I'm glad I at least have an ocean view, even if it is shoddy. Not much mud yet... so it's still very early.

The worst is coming—one of the only things I'm sure of. Narrowly avoided getting tossed in the cells after becoming involved with Theia. Word has gotten out about her escape. It's only a matter of time until she's found. Let's see what this screwed-up night brings.

-C

Their conversation came to a halt when a large tail disrupted the stillness of the waters outside. Warm wind blew stronger against the cracked window, carrying a high-pitched whistling. Castin moved to the other side of the room to retrieve his armor from a closet. There were no other colors on the rusty hangers besides gray. He zipped, clipped, and secured his entire protective getup, preparing to head outside before the imminent threat became more prevalent.

"So, what do we need to take care of now?" Castin asked, adjusting his gear.

"By the thirteenth section, there is a package that has almost fallen off of the ledge," Ezra explained. "It hasn't gone completely over by sheer luck. It's caught on its handle and dangling over a pack of... something. One wrong step and we could fall down into them, but we really need what's in there. I've already wasted enough time trying to take care of it by myself. The others won't agree to join."

"'We'? Why can't whoever else needs it help you?" Castin checked over all his chrome guns, strapping them to each limb, and smiled at the sight of his freshly reloaded pistol. He glanced out of the room's window at a group who were sitting around and talking. "Let me guess, they're scared to shoot? They gotta get comfortable with using real and effective firearms."

I nudged his notebook away from me and spoke up. "Let's just go get the bag while we still can."

"So, you're tagging along, but not *really* helping?" Castin asked, eyeing the knife I was given with a grin.

"I'll be there as a spotter in case either of you slip." I swiftly undid the retractable blade. "I can defend up close with this if needed. I'm also grateful for it as I don't believe in using guns, I'd choose the other side."

Castin looked at Ezra. "Are you alright with that?"

He shrugged. "I'm not sure why you ask everyone for their opinions on sides. I don't care. It's his choice."

"You want to gamble your life with what, a butter knife? Whatever." Castin scoffed as he led the way out of the disorganized room. "Maybe you should learn about our currency so you can purchase something useful, like a gun. You'd have to save for a long time."

This guy's a broken record. I chose to stay quiet.

No one spoke for a minute. Ezra awkwardly started counting his ammo as we made it out of the hallways and into what was hardly considered fresher air. I inhaled deeply and tried to keep breathing steadily. *Stay collected no matter what happens.*

We reached the twelfth part of the gate and crawled to get to the thirteenth portion. Part of the structure was falling apart at its base. Mud, rocks, and branches were exposed, growing out from the concrete. The bright red box was easy to spot as it rocked back and forth in the muggy wind. Ezra had explained that the bag contained medical supplies, bandages, and ointment, but most importantly, a bottle of prescription pills that were urgently needed.

The bag dangled just above a pack of hostile semiaquatic mutants that roamed the mud in search of things to devour. They hissed as they climbed on top of one another, clawing at the dirt and making more of it collapse as they fought relentlessly to reach the top.

The oversized salamanders were knee height and had around eight stringy tentacles extending from their backs and arms. Their eyes were a light gold, each had speckled skin, marked with various hues, and was covered in what appeared to be infected welts.

Each had sharp, curved claws that were a sickly green and left holes in the mud as they tore away at the already *very* unstable foundation.

"Woah! I can't even count how many there are!" Castin exclaimed as he stepped closer, shooting at them with his pistol. He didn't miss a single shot.

I stayed near the gate, not touching the metal as I could practically feel the heat radiating from it. Sweat dripped into my eyes as I kept a lookout mostly for Ezra, who was hyping himself up to leave the safety bounds to go and retrieve the medicine package.

"I can do this! I have to do this! Think of Emery!" He paced back and forth nervously while yelling out loud to himself, "She needs this before the infection worsens!"

The moon was not only keeping the horrendous mutants well-lit but also Castin's annoyed frown as he reloaded his gun. "Hurry up, man! Get moving!"

"I'm trying!" Ezra shouted. He held his breath as he stepped down, concerned solely on the first aid kit. With a carefully placed lunge, he managed to grab onto the handle and slide it over his wrist. "Keep firing!"

Castin switched to using his compact submachine gun. "You don't have to tell me that!"

The mutants squirmed and writhed around, some already dead underneath the rest, but a startling number were beginning to make their way up the mud, just below where I was observing.

My body went cold once I got a nearby look at them. "They're getting too close!" I warned Castin.

"Wow! Really? Why don't you actually do something then?" he snapped in response.

I began stabbing at their grotesque faces, my leather armor keeping my skin protected from their stings.

"I can make it back fast!" Ezra shouted and gripped a thick root that stuck out with his free hand.

Those who refused to help were watching from inside, unable to pry their eyes away from the danger their friend faced to help them.

I need to come more prepared on the next mission!

Castin shot at a few more near his feet. "Screw this!" He pulled a forest green hand grenade from one of his holsters, removed the safety clip, and tossed it ahead, watching as it exploded only seconds later.

Ezra wasted no time using the extra space to maneuver back. "I got it! Thank you both!"

We all returned to safety, letting out sighs of relief as the few remaining creatures wandered off in search of something else to eat, screeching atrociously as they disappeared into the distance. Some of them, driven by desperate hunger, began to bite into each other's parasitic and diseased flesh. Trails of their corrosive blood dripped into their muddy footsteps as they retreated.

I held out my hand to guide Ezra as he stepped back through the gate, ensuring he was safely inside on both feet. "Glad you're okay and that we could help you out with this. I hope to never face those repulsive things again. I'm around to assist, though, if needed. We did the best we could despite the risks."

"'We'?" Castin snickered. "What did you even do?"

Ezra, clad in an armored fisherman's outfit with numerous external pockets, took a few minutes to collect two handfuls of small and medium-sized screws stowed away in some of the compartments. "Here are the rest of the bay dollars I have left as a reward for you two. Thank you for helping me with this. I'll go get these pills delivered to the others. Stay safe out here." He handed us the reward and then headed back to where everyone else was staying to deliver the kit.

I examined the screws in my hands, quickly counting them. *This probably won't be enough for anything substantial. I have to get more.*

"Now that everything here is settled... I have other tasks to complete." Castin was already a few steps away, his hat concealing whatever look of judgment he was probably giving me, "Maybe you can make yourself more useful next time? Guess we'll see."

"Before you leave, I've been meaning to speak with you about Theia getting out. Word is spreading around." I spoke quickly to keep his attention, mentioning her name had caught it, but it also seemed as if he appeared fretful when taking a slow step back.

He frowned from under his hat. "Uh... she'll be caught soon for her wrongdoings. My crew with the Emergency Biohazard team will make sure no one is put in danger or harm's way. Don't worry."

"I'm not." *She's not who we need to fear.* "I was actually wondering if you had anything to do with her escaping the cell block earlier? Does the work you all conduct have anything to do with Magic Wielders?" *He knows that I've been one, I hope that the smoke doesn't return from my hands. I don't want my supernatural abilities back to make me feel less human again.*

"My work here is confidential. I'll just say that I keep things running smoothly by cleaning up messes left behind by the reckless outsiders." Castin almost touched his hat to see me fully but pulled his fingers away at the last second. "Magic Wielders. Those who cause destruction with spells and wield weapons that not only side with destruction, but also confusion."

"Are the problems between these weapon dealers *that* awful? Your opinions seem biased. Sounds like the Frontier had some crumbling from within to cause a social divide like this." I looked up at the moon and everything it brightened, mostly the Loot Vaults.

Castin nodded and side-eyed my navy blue and brown outfit with a grimace. "Glad you're following, but not closely enough. You should ditch that blade in your holster. Ignorance will get you killed. Apparently, you don't stand with anyone either. When problems unravel, and they will, you'll want to know exactly what you stand for. You can't remain neutral for long. Not with this much at stake."

Clouds moved lazily across the sky, covering the moon as our conversation grew rigid. I took a few steps backward when I noticed others approaching us from the direction of the residential rooms.

"There's no problem here," I said authoritatively to the group wearing various shades of gray that had gathered behind Castin with their guns drawn.

"Have you seen where the woman who escaped is?" they asked. "We're on the lookout for her."

"He hasn't," Castin answered for me before I had the chance to speak. "There's a lot he doesn't know."

Then, out of the corner of my eye, I saw Theia hiding behind a drive-in theater sign... and she saw me too.

THEIA

Night

CHAPTER SIX: TRUST FALL

IT FELT AS THOUGH EVERYONE WAS TALKING about, speculating, and searching for me. *I'm so glad Zekiel didn't give me away to the Biohazard guards.* I'd tried to sidestep their extensive search with a racing heart after escaping the cell block. The research agency called 'The Frontier' had forced me there after discovering more than they originally knew about my past before Salt Crest. I had been brought to the city against my will in the first place, though, so *that* wasn't what surprised me. What caught me off guard was how quickly I became a disposable threat to them, despite their initial desperation for my involvement.

My right forefinger used to hold immense power. I had become known by many for my ability to harness teleportation for others and myself on rare occasions. Even though I was somehow granted such a unique gift, it often made me feel detached from myself.

Upon deciding to enter a wondrous portal with Aadavan and Lorelai, two of the most important people to me, I had altered my life forever. Not only had they each lost their lives on the unknown planet that we encountered, but there was a shadowy ache of regret that had lingered with me ever since.

I wasn't sure how to live with myself after being complicit in the wrongdoings that took place there. I had no way to explain to anyone else what was really going on in my mind as it fell apart. At first, I didn't notice how cold and desensitized I had become, avoiding the right choices.

After unspeakable things unfolded at that triangular arena, filled with cursed nature and planetary fighters facing their problems head-on or running from them, I was somehow one of the few who survived and made it back to Earth for good.

Asperhill, my quaint and secluded home, no longer felt like where I belonged. Part of my mind was forever lost in what felt like a dreamland of mistakes. I wasn't lonely, though. Elijah was still alive and shared a connection with me.

We always seemed to find each other.

When the Frontier had subdued and brought me to Salt Crest, Elijah arrived too after agreeing to help Tule with her plans. *It means so much that he voted for me to walk free at the sentencing.* He had my back even though I had once failed to have his. I wanted to help other Magic Wielders, not hurt or let anyone down, but due to Forced Evolutionary Magic, I did exactly that and now faced the consequences.

After escaping the cell block by taking Tule's keys, I'd mostly hid in graffiti-covered alleyways. *How can I convince the others that I don't deserve the death penalty?*

I still hadn't told Castin that my teleportation spell wasn't working, no matter how much I focused on bringing it to life. Despite his gossiping getting me in at first, he came around later and tried to work together by bringing me some sort of special armor set. It didn't grant me back the power I used to have.

Instead, it gave me the use of invisibility and I wasn't sure at all what to do with that in the long run. I wasn't looking forward to telling him this since the list of others who I had already disappointed was long enough.

I tried my best not to run into anyone on the busy streets. I had to keep reactivating my special spell, as its duration lasted only thirty seconds each time. Posters had been put up all over the city with my face and an alarming message on them that painted me as a 'sinister' criminal. *Can't believe there's a reward for whoever finds me.*

At least I got a sword before I became the villain in almost everyone's eyes. A kind and thoughtful man who called himself the Librarian had generously helped me afford what I needed to defend myself, then I was determined to have more training in combat.

While going invisible was useful for hiding, it wouldn't be able to get me as far as my usual gift. Through meditation, I had once been able to perform magic of unprecedented strength, which had made me feel special and irreplaceable. It used to only take me a minute to completely change, or save, the life of another with my gift. But I had devastatingly lost it.

Unfortunately, my nerves were never the same after involving myself with certain substances, and the damage had been made worse by the thin mattress in my cell. Pins and needles invasively had traveled through me since my cliffside injury. I'd fallen onto a rocky surface and hit the ground after using a command against my will.

Ever since then, I've had periods of numbness in my limbs, and each day it became more challenging to feel temperature changes. No one else knew about my nerve damage, just as they didn't know about my inability to wield specific abilities.

My mind and heart felt numb too. I wasn't sure if my body would ever work the same way again. I found it hard to love myself for who I was because of the person I had once been. The damage I succumbed to had maimed me for life, and the emotional and physical scars were a constant reminder of my failures. I was always on the verge of tears, no matter what was happening. The ache within me would never go away.

The other person who I knew might understand my feelings was Elijah, someone I'd never been able to forget, despite countless sleepless nights trying to. He used to go by the name Cloudburst to conceal his identity. We shared a connection that no one else seemed to experience. I had involuntarily stepped into his mind and heard his thoughts, leaving him with no privacy whenever I was close by. I had even been able to speak to him without saying anything aloud.

Though I wanted to keep our past behind closed doors... Elijah didn't seem able to. A few times, I'd seen him speaking with others while glancing at me from the corner of his eye. He couldn't stop looking at me whenever our paths almost crossed. *Not sure I'll ever believe that no part of Elijah wants vengeance for the unforgettable connection I was forced to have over him. What is he saying to others? Will I ever find out?*

I could no longer hear his thoughts, but whenever he saw me, there was a look in his eyes that suggested he still believed I could. *He can't hear mine now, right?*

I was able to stay under the radar until I accidentally ran into a group of citygoers near the drive-in just as my invisibility wore off. They were wearing futuristic dark and light gray outfits and equipped with many guns. Crows adorned their sleeves, symbols I recognized from Castin's tattoos, the same markings of those who had forced me into a portal and from the library.

"You don't make any rules here! We do!" a stranger told me angrily as they tucked a pack of cigarettes into their chest pocket.

"I-I don't want problems," I stammered, keeping my hands away from my sword to avoid making matters worse, though I couldn't stop myself from shaking.

"Then don't create more," another warned.

"If you do? We'll take matters into our own hands." All of them stared at my right index finger before I quickly hid it. "We aren't afraid to make you pay for what you did. According to those recordings, there are almost twenty-four hours left until some sort of storm kills us. Think you can manage to not torture or destroy anyone else's life before then?"

I was on the verge of breaking down in distress, feeling as though my life was spiraling more and more out of control. I needed help from someone who truly cared for me, but I didn't want to ask for it. I didn't want to appear weak. I saw my shadow on the ground, slouched and worn out, reflecting my worry and lack of energy.

Desperately, I glanced down at my finger, hoping a teleportation command would get me out of this mess. *Please! Please just work again! I need to feel like myself!*

"Wait a second! Why are you looking at your hand like that?" one of them demanded and pointed at it.

"Are you about to do something?" another asked.

They aimed their guns at me, their vicious glares on the narrow road. I could've sworn I was standing on puddles of dried blood, which I only noticed after avoiding eye contact with everyone. *Who knows what happened here before I arrived? Who the Frontier really is? What if they created the curses that ruined my life? Did they make F.E.M.? What if the 'F' isn't for 'Forced', but, 'Frontier'? Is E.M. another group? Evolutionary M–*

Elijah came around the concrete corner near us, it was clear he was searching. "Theia! What's going on?"

I felt a lump in my throat at the sound of his voice. *He's probably been looking around everywhere for me.* I was sick to my stomach at his arrival, yet curious. *But for what reason? Revenge? Bay dollars? Does he care?*

"We're handling things!" a masked woman snapped before aiming her gun and firing at me. I managed to turn invisible again just in time to get away from them.

"Where is she?" another shouted. "You will pay!"

"Just leave her alone," Elijah intervened. They eyed the highly sought-after sword secured to his back.

The blade had multiple mysterious curves, a brown leather handle, and was a cool silver.

"Why would we do that?" she retorted angrily.

Elijah glanced around as he replied, "There's a lot you don't know. I can tell by the threats you recklessly spew. If you kill Theia, you'll ruin everything. You also won't be alive much longer."

A masked man, the same height as him, got close to his face. "How about not interfering with matters that don't have anything to do with you?"

"I don't need to explain myself. I also don't want to stand around arguing with those who are committed to misunderstanding the knowledge I share. Time is too valuable for that nonsense." With that, Elijah turned and followed me with determination as I headed to the outskirts.

I already knew he would do everything he could to track me down and speak to me again. *But what if he wants something from me? An apology? What else?*

It was only the two of us in the scorching night by the gate's edge, staring at the still water as my power fully wore off. I could be seen again. I felt incredibly vulnerable, especially around him, and I wanted nothing more than to be left entirely alone. I knew he'd also never forget what happened between us. Seeing him beside me made the past feel all too real.

"Elijah?" My voice was deeper than usual, barely above a whisper. "Why did you help me back there?"

He took a few steps closer, and I backed up with each one. "Because you can't die, Theia, and you have no idea how to defend yourself from their attacks." His hair was much shorter, but when I saw his face even nearer it was exactly as I remembered.

"You've got me. I have nowhere to run or hide." I raised my hands as if surrendering. Guilt felt like a life sentence, no matter what I did, or what I chose to say.

One of Elijah's swords was similar to mine, and he also wore only black. "I'm not after you for revenge if that's what you're thinking, okay? Please don't worry that I'm here to ever hurt you, Theia. It's just that you have no idea how valuable your armor is. It might be special. It could save us, and you already know something about doing that."

"Wait..." I paused, gathering my thoughts. "How are you able to speak with me right now? After everything we've been through together?"

"You let me go back to my home freely. Ever since then, I haven't been able to get my mind off of you.

The impact you've had on me. You manifested our meeting at the castle. Love is a powerful force, and it happens for a reason. Maybe it was predestined."

He has it wrong. I felt my stomach tighten. *What he feels for me can't be any form of love, just like it wasn't when he tried to get closer before. I have to change the subject.* I wanted to be free too, which meant wrestling with my desire to avoid Elijah as much as I could.

"I have something to share." I looked at the motionless ocean and extended my finger. "It's not working. The others might kill me if they find out. It might be related to what happened on that planet."

"Are you serious? What happened… when?" Elijah asked with concern as he kept from touching it.

It took a moment for me to compose myself and keep my tears at bay. "I was injured when you weren't around. I fell on my tailbone near the ocean. A planetary fighter—you'd recognize her—dropped me while forcing a teleportation command reversal. I'm lucky I wasn't killed. Only what I had which was unique kept me alive…" my voice trailed off brokenly.

"I had no idea you were by yourself when I saw you at Asperhill. We don't have to discuss what happened to the others, okay? I'm sorry to hear about your fall." He then tried to persuade again, "You may think that you can't help me, but you can try. Why not remove the armor piece so someone else can then?"

"I can't. Some sort of force is keeping it on." I tried to pull it off again. "But I need it. I can't hold my own in combat anyway. I'll take all the help I can get."

Elijah's voice took on a seductive tone. "I could help you take it off... Then help you take your mind off things for a bit before we see what else it can do?"

I stood in shock as he placed his fingers on my arm, trailing them upwards until he reached the part where there was no leather and his skin touched mine. I shivered and quickly shook my head. "No."

He backed away and nodded. "I'll respect that."

"Can you teach me how to fight, though? Between the past and present, I'll never be short on enemies, I need to know what to do." I felt disheartened.

Elijah paused longer than usual, lost in thought before answering. "Alright. Almost everyone is asleep. Let's go to the training quarters across from the Sea Bartering shop. It's two streets away from the cell block, but don't worry, I'll make sure they don't try to put you there again."

"Really?" I felt a sense of camaraderie between us.

"Yeah. I'll keep a lookout in case anything doesn't seem right nearby." He began to lead the way for me.

We walked side by side, our voices were quiet and steps in unison. The storefront lights led us to the vacant quarters. Spending time with him felt forbidden, but his help was something I desperately needed.

"What about what you can't see?" I continued, "When someone is attacking you, sometimes you may not see them, but great fighters can sense it. They know *just* when to turn and how to block a stealthy attack. What about in the darkness? How do you sharpen your senses for that?"

"Skills become muscle memory," Elijah explained as the armory and residing rooms came into view, one street away from our destination. "We'll make it out of this alive too, okay? I could spend the rest of my life paying you back for what you did for me in the past. No one else knows our story, the full one, but what matters is that we do."

I evaded looking him in the eyes, unsure if he'd see the guilt that I carried in mine.

Once we reached the training arena, Elijah walked around the space and surveyed the equipment. There were levels of stairs for us to practice on, bathed in moonlight that highlighted the magical top and black leathers I wore. Beads of sweat trickled down my face as I tied my braids up with achy arms.

"Let's start simple with stretching," Elijah said.

After that, his basic instructions became complex as we trained over the next few hours. When he tried to get close and place a hand on my back, I glanced over my shoulder and saw Zekiel walking by through a damaged window. I sidestepped away from his second attempted advance, relieved by the interruption.

"I have to hide because he and Tule haven't seen me since I escaped or know I have the key!" I lied about the first part—I knew that Zekiel was aware of my presence—but the second half was true. I wasn't sure what would happen if more information got out about me. I had something almost everyone else wanted and might kill for.

"I'll talk to him as a distraction, okay?" Elijah said, trying to stay calm. "Head in the opposite direction at the gate, remain quiet, and I'll meet you there soon."

"Okay." I followed him outside and bolted away as quickly as possible, trying to stay out of Zekiel's line of sight. *Maybe he's trying to talk to me as a trick to turn me in? He's probably desperate for bay dollars. I would be too if I didn't have something to protect myself with.*

I used invisibility from the armor as often as possible when its effects didn't need time to recharge yet stayed within hearing range to know what they were conversing about from a distance.

"What brings you out here?" Elijah asked Zekiel as he leaned against a rusty column.

"I was wondering if you would work with Tule and me to increase our chances of survival? She and I know you're close with Theia and have experience with magic. We've just learned some information that you may find useful. We need a specific piece of armor so that she can bring us home, it has to be tested out."

I found it impossible to not move slower so that I could hear them better. I hardly paid attention to my surroundings as I walked along the gate sections.

Elijah kept his response brief, "What exactly are you asking of me right now? Do you have this item?"

"No. Tule thought she knew where it was, but what she found turned out to just be a regular set. Theia most likely has it, which helped her escape. We need you to tell us what you know and get her to agree to our plans. Then everyone who is here against their will can be saved by being teleported to safety."

"We aren't allied enough for me to trust you like this, alright?" Elijah responded as I expected him to.

I stayed close by after passing the Sea Bartering shop and leaned back against the metal gate, still keeping an eye on the two men under the dim lights.

For a few moments, there was only silence until Elijah took hold of his sword and pointed the hilt toward Zekiel. He kept his arm outstretched until it was taken from him. "I need to get rid of this. Keep it. I have another to use instead. *That's* the help I'll give."

"Do you know how much this costs?" Zekiel asked, incredulous. "Thank you. I'll never forget your help."

"At least I know that with you, this weapon may be put to good use. It will be helpful against whatever else is in the darkness. You and Tule should remain careful. I'm going to keep searching for more answers. I'll also keep my matters with Theia private."

"If you save us? I promise the credit will go to you," Zekiel assured. "I hope the same will be done for me. I'll do the best I can to save who I'm able to."

I watched as their conversation came to an end, drawing near to what I thought was the sixteenth section, and leaned back against the gate as I waited for Elijah. I rested my arms in between the middle poles without looking at them, hardly able to feel the torrid heat that zapped everyone else's skin if they accidentally touched it.

"You were right. It was Zekiel. He tried to get me to agree to help him and Tule. Without you knowing, of course." Elijah had made his way over to me around the shadowy corner and told me what I already knew.

"They don't trust me, and I'm not surprised." His words should've greatly worried me, but I always tried to understand where others were coming from. I knew that there was a gray area and that people could change. "Paranoia broke out about the past. I can understand why some fearfully wanted to take a vote."

"It was hypocritical of Tule to try to make people listen to her views and warnings about magic, but then also reprimand someone for a history of using the same magic. Do you get what I'm saying?" He was tense.

"Elijah... It's okay. I'm not upset with her about anything." My voice was tired. "I know that she's just doing her job."

After several minutes of trying, I was still unable to get the armor piece off. I figured that something else was needed, to tap into an energy source to remove it, but there were no current clues as to what it could be.

"Try not to worry about it," Elijah finally said to me after waiting as long as he could. "I'm sure it will come off when the time is right. Though there's one thing I want to check if you don't mind me looking down the back to see if something's embedded in it."

My heart raced as I leaned against the gate once more, going backward a little further this time. "N-no."

"Why?" Elijah walked closer under the moonlight.

I tried to move away from him but stumbled backward before I could even respond. I cried out for help as I lost my balance and grip on the jagged metal in front of me. As I fell, I came to a haunting realization. *This is the thirteenth section!*

"Theia!" Elijah yelled after me, avoiding any contact with the gate while leaning over and watching.

I painfully landed on my back in the mud. It began bubbling before I sat up, then sank downwards, engulfing my entire body before I was able to let out another scream. My vision was obscured by mud falling into my tear-filled eyes.

Then the Librarian ran over, holding a book in one hand, and a sword in the other. He stood heroically in the windy night.

Then it faded to black.

THE LIBRARIAN

Early Morning

24 hours remaining

CHAPTER SEVEN: AN OPEN BOOK

BEFORE ENTERING THE SEA-LIKE WASTELAND my life always revolved around routines. Reading had been my great escape from the mundane. That, and drugs. I had to stop using some to sell them, and in doing so, entered a realm that I thought only existed in fictional stories. One typical weekday, my friends had asked if I wanted to search for treasure. Videos had been going viral about a conspiracy theory involving a certain publisher, claiming that the books they had released contained hidden clues leading to secret locations where vast amounts of money, advanced technology, and weapons had been buried. They usually didn't invite me to join them, knowing I preferred to stay home, but they recognized one of the book covers as something notable I had read before.

"We *need* you to come with us to investigate this!" My friend's voice had crackled due to the phone's weak reception. "I swear it's t-the same book! There's no way you can pass on this opportunity!"

She had been right. I placed a bookmark in the memoir I could hardly stop reading to give them my full attention. A main enjoyment of mine was finding and trading goods, especially with big rewards. "What did you say the title was again?" *I have to make su—*

"'The Vaults'. There are purple clouds over gray buildings which appear surrounded by barbed wire." Her voice tapered off eerily, almost as if surprised by it.

That all sounds right. It might be the other half of the duology I've been looking for. If it's four, two, nine then I'll know for sure. This might be the guide that can take my F.E.M. commands further. I may finally be able to find the vaults. "What are the last three digits of its ISBN?"

"Um, I dunno, lemme check again." There had been a pause.

I'd waited patiently in silence for her response.

"Four, two, and nine."

"On my way." I hung up the phone abruptly, avoiding telling others 'goodbye' as much as possible since I remained hopeful to see them again, and they had understood that. After putting my glasses on, I grabbed my book bag and a few other things, then headed out the front door.

It normally took much more convincing for me to leave my house and join them, but I had made it to the address I was eventually texted within the next hour. I had been told to meet them in a complicated forest that I'd never ventured far into before. Sometimes we'd stop there to hang out and share a few smokes, but we'd never stayed past the golden hour. When it had grown dark outside, we would typically head back home.

I had been the last to arrive in the nearly empty parking lot, where my friends were huddled together, excitedly guessing what kinds of hidden treasures we were about to uncover.

"Hey." I approached them in a hurry, securing my books and making sure my car was locked. *I won't get my hopes up too high. We may find nothing, but at least I can be here to help in case things take a wrong turn.*

"Finally!" My friend had exclaimed, Em's tone mirroring that of our phone call. She'd nodded at Matt, who'd seemed to be nearly out of patience.

"The Librarian has arrived!" he'd declared, waving his arms in the air. "We're losing daylight by the minute—let's go!"

As we headed onto the main hiking trail and got our bearings, a few of them had told me about what they'd seen on the news about magic... and the similarities between it and what I'd seemed to know. Clues were revealed, some I previously refrained from sharing.

Apparently, the book I had read was a limited-edition copy, one of only six ever printed. This information had been new to me, but it hadn't made much sense, because the copy I'd purchased was one of at least twenty on the crowded and well-stocked shelves of a locally owned bookstore.

We continued to walk further into the unknown, trees growing taller and thicker with each dark mile, I had been asked a series of questions to guide the way.

A sense of unease had begun to stir inside of me as I'd trailed a bit farther behind everyone else. *I don't think we are being led to valuables...*

Everyone had started heading down an extremely narrow path that split into two.

I'd stepped off to explore the side they'd chosen to avoid, curiosity pulling me in and a faint sense of magic lingering in the air. "I'll rejoin you all in a minute, okay? I think there might be something useful over here worth investigating." I'd called back, giving them a quick heads-up before fully departing. None of them had seemed interested in joining my search.

After pushing my glasses up the bridge of my nose, I pulled out a flashlight from my satchel, which had been mostly filled with books, pens, lighters, and joints, to illuminate my surroundings. The sun had fully set, and the warm light from the bulb revealed the sycamore trees nearly embracing either side of the path as I'd stepped deeper into the woods.

That's when my life was forever changed.

I dropped what I'd been holding when I saw a portal forming out of thin air, spinning with stars. I had been entranced by the sight and turned to tell my friends, but it started to close before I could reach them.

What if I'm meant to go inside? I wondered why it had appeared before me. I took a firm grip on my bag's canvas handle to bring it while stepping in.

A few weeks later, things went from bad to worse.

For the second time in my life, it felt as though time stood completely still. What I thought would be a regular night of slinging goods had rapidly transformed into a dire rescue mission. A woman I'd recently befriended, Theia, needed my help as she was yanked down into the depths of a muddy abyss.

Elijah, someone I'd met at the library not too long before, stood to my right, his voice barely a whisper. I tried to reassure him that I would help. But with each second, she was forcibly dragged deeper below through narrow, wet tunnels leading to a place no one had ever escaped—an oceanic labyrinth of woven passageways, dead ends, and limited pockets of air.

The tunnels of Crow Library.

"I have to rescue her!" Elijah shouted, his voice cracking with desperation. "But the storm! I still need to find another way to help everyone in this city!"

I tightened the hold I had on each weapon in my hands. "All my hours of reading have prepared me for this. I'm going to rescue her. You should stay up here."

At that moment, the sound of a gun being reloaded came from near the Sea Bartering shop, followed by the thud of Castin's boots. "What's all this commotion about? I can hardly get any sleep."

I waved my arms to get his immediate attention and loudly told him, "Theia's fallen into the tunnels!"

"What?" Castin's tone shifted as he took off his hat and ran a hand through his hair. "Didn't know it was *this* bad!"

"I'm going after her! You need to stay up here and search for anything that can help the others!" I instructed Elijah. "You're one of the few who can find the key in nature if you use Crow Library's texts!"

"I'll go with you to help," Castin stated, as if there was another reason why he felt compelled to join. He seemed almost too calm. "Elijah, can you please keep my hat for me? You can't lose it. Alright?"

Elijah didn't say anything else after agreeing to hold onto it for him, and the two of us headed out of the city's bounds. *At least my bag is near the shop up here.* We raced toward a different tunnel entrance that had bubbled open as the other closed. I made sure my jacket's buttons were fastened all the way and jumped inside, thankful for the tool I had with me—a book of commands with extraordinary ink that allowed me to read was written in the dark. It was something others may not give a second thought to, but they were bonded and couldn't work without the other.

Castin jumped in moments after me, and we each hit the ground not far apart. The impact knocked the air out of my lungs. It was pitch black, and the only sound aside from our labored gasps for air was droplets of water falling into a small puddle nearby.

"Are you alright?" I asked him once I was able to get to my feet, hunched over and touching the muddy wall beside me to orient myself.

"Yeah. I've had worse days if you could believe it." Castin seethed in pain from landing on a few of his weapons. "Glad I left my hat with Elijah, though."

I was thankful to have landed on my hands and knees, my sword sheathed securely behind me. Nothing had fallen out of my coat either. My ink bottle was intact. "We're going to have to use magic to survive here."

"Ah, so just like everywhere else? This comes as *such* a shock," he responded sarcastically.

Water dripped in the dark, and I felt goosebumps ripple over my skin from the cold. "Yes, but in more... unexpected ways."

"These sounds might drive me crazy," Castin muttered. "Had no idea we could walk around down here."

The tunnel slowly began filling with droplets of warm water from what was once the salty sea. Creatures slithered through the mud passageways. I did my best to avoid touching the walls.

"How are we supposed to see anything?" Castin asked.

I thought aloud, "I never thought I'd need to use this combination before, but now's as good a time as any, I suppose. Let's see if I can recall the sequence..."

I pulled the small notebook and feather quill with a round bottle from my pockets. With a steady grip, I untied the tiny rope that secured the lid and dipped the mythical pen in. A drop of ink pooled into the tip, and I dragged it across an empty page:

F.E.M.: LightBook

The paper began to glow as I wrote, even though the final letter was nearly halfway off the edge. A grainy yellow light instantly brightened up the sunken space.

"We'll only have light for so long. It's sort of like a flashlight; it will run out of batteries, so to speak," I explained.

"So, you'll just write another word in it, right?" Castin asked.

"Hopefully, if nothing happens to the ink. This type of journal is completely useless without it." I secured the feather and book back in their respective pockets and moved past Castin to a passageway in the ground. "See this? We'll have to crawl through. Let's hope she's on the other side. Theia, we're coming to get you!" I called out loudly before stepping down into the next entrance.

The second tunnel we entered was much larger, the mud extremely wet, and it presented a new issue. Three different pathways diverged from where we stood. The LightBook's glow revealed unsettling characteristics of the mud around us. Almost every inch of the nearby surface looked to be pulsating on its own, and a few palm-sized rocks had been forcefully pushed out by something on the other side.

I examined each sewer-like opening and thought out loud to myself, "Splitting up would be a terrible idea. We'd probably never find one another again."

"You should write down a teleportation phrase," Castin suggested.

"No offense, but that's not a good idea either," I said. "Certain spells shouldn't be used without guidance. We could end up worse off."

"Theia?" Castin called out into the far-left entrance. "Where are you?"

"We'll have to take risks to save her. We need to start searching through one out of these three current options. Let's hope everything goes successfully up above in the meantime." I pointed at each of our next potential destinations. "We have to keep moving. No matter what's happening, we can't stay in one spot."

"Let's go down the middle one," Castin suggested.

I reopened my booklet and carefully wrote the keyphrase again. The glow intensified as its internal clock started counting down how long the light would last. The previous page darkened, eventually matching the ones before it as the life inside of the paper faded.

"The checkered floors in Crow Library were designed intentionally. Each square represents a different tunnel that trails deep down. I'd truly be surprised if Theia is s-still alive." My voice was unsteady. *I have to see her and my other friends again; we all need to be reunited. I'll make it happen.* "Let's hope she at least fell into a section with a pocket of air, away from anything else living."

Castin went through the middle tunnel first as I held the light above him, though it didn't fully reveal what was below. I heard his muddy steps, the sides of his armor scraping against the narrow passageway, and then a muffled scream for help when he reached the bottom.

"What's wrong?!" I leaned over with my book in hand to see what had happened. "Are you alright?"

I gasped in terror at the mangled sight before me.

Castin stood next to a trembling stranger covered in dirt, his left leg impaled by a sharp spike sticking out of the mud. Blood poured down the side of the metal and his exposed tibia bone. "I don't know how long I've been here, please help me!"

"I'm jumping down!"

Then Castin stepped out of the way and pulled part of the spike to the side so I wouldn't land on it too. Luckily, he had missed it by only a few inches. I reached the bottom with a loud thud, wincing at the fall's impact and strain on my lower back.

"I have to write a command to heal you," I told the wounded man who lay sprawled out. "Okay?"

He shook in agony from within an almost completely mud-covered, full-body suit. "Do it, please!"

I coated the tip in ink once more and turned to the next blank page. "There's only one catch… this booklet can only cast one power at a time. Once I change it, it can never go back to doing what it had done before."

Neither the stranger nor Castin said anything.

So, I sent a command for health kits in the dark.

Suddenly, there was a loud splash somewhere close by. *What was that?* I began scribbling a line of words as the wounded stranger's breath rattled and he continued to lose blood. *I have to move as fast as possible!* The pages in my hands began glowing red, allowing me to see what I wrote:

F.E.M.: RestoreHealth

I approached the man, who could barely keep his eyes open, and held the book near his side. Floating specks of purple, snowflake-shaped particles fell over his leg, putting it back together and restoring the damaged body part right before our eyes. The blood loss came to a halt. The layers of his flesh, muscles, and nerves were woven and stitched together like a neatly crocheted fabric. The soft blur in the tunnel disappeared as the healing potion depleted its resources. I sighed in relief. *I'm so glad that worked, I don't know what else we would've done.*

Magic had been useful to me many times before, which is why I researched it extensively. Drugs were my gateway into the magical realm. They led me down a path that made me realize my wildest dreams. What I wanted to do was help others, no matter what sacrifice it took, even if it meant them getting the quick fix or escapism they needed.

"Thank you so much!" the stranger exclaimed.

I helped him up to his feet. "You're welcome."

"Can you only do that one time?" Castin asked, motioning for me to step aside with him for a moment.

"No, I can create health potions infinitely. That *is* until I need to use the book for something else. Let's hope I don't have to switch the power from this one." I kept the knowledge I had about my other manuscripts to myself, I didn't want to overwhelm him with endless information about the different spells they can cast.

I struggled to see his expression as he stated, "Sounds like you're messing with Forced Evolutionary Magic. The others don't have to know, and I don't care. Now let's keep going. Can't stay here any longer."

Doesn't this guy work for the Frontier? Why does he not care at all? I'm surprised he's not questioning me.

The fact that I had quite extensive experience in F.E.M. was something I kept to myself. Only Theia had seen a page with some of my drafted commands that I accidentally left open while we were together in the library. She tried to question me about it, but I asked her to keep it to herself. I kept the law at bay as much as possible, wearing black to display my opposition to their forces. I stood by magic because it had been there for me when no one else was, even the kind we were told was 'wrong.' *Just depends on how we use it.* It made me want to be there for others and help them escape.

After Castin stepped away from me, the man I healed came over to shake my hand while still catching his breath. "Thank you again. I've been down here for a while after getting s-separated from my team."

*I know what it's like to not have your group around.
I'm sorry to hear he's going through something similar.*
"You're welcome. I'm just glad I could help out,
honestly. How are you feeling? Any pain?"

The stranger took a few seconds to respond,
assessing his leg. "I don't have any. Thank you for
asking. How about I join you both through these
tunnels? I may be able to find my coworkers. They're
probably worried about me. I'm Theo, by the way."

"I know the feeling," I forced a half-hearted shrug,
as the faces of those I cared about flashed in my mind.
*His name is so similar to Theia's. I hope she knows that
I'm going to rescue her.* "Nice to meet you, Theo. You
can call me the Librarian. My acquaintance Castin and
I will help protect you. Do you have any weap–?"

"No," Theo replied, shivering at the memory.
"Some insane Drifters—lawless criminals with no
purpose in life—stole them from me on their way to
their campout spot. They're the ones who put this
spike down here as a trap in the first place."

The three of us searched the nearby darkness
before moving forward as the glow from my book
resumed, even after the entire duration of healing. I
used it to check through the center of the middle
tunnel until the brightness completely faded. I lowered

my legs onto the mud when a few bubbles began popping. Then, there was rumbling. *This can't be good.*

"Below my feet!" Castin shouted unexpectedly. "I just felt something move down below! Stay alert!"

I felt most of the mud under my heavy boots crumbling and rattling as there was movement throughout it. A knot grew in my stomach and I had a hard time breathing due to the sudden stress. The tunnel's stability was compromised as a mutated mud leech tore through it, emerging towards our feet. I had never seen such a nightmare-inducing monster before, only in fictitious stories, but now I was face to face with a real one.

I became dizzy at the prospect of fighting it, thinking about what I'd read before about certain spells that could help us. *If only I had some of my other books with me!* They each granted a wide array of awe-inspiring uses, but I only had one in my coat at the time that could bring those powers to life. *I'll do the best I can!*

Everything continued rumbling around us as the creature squirmed around ferociously. It was hunting for blood, its three jaws extended. Despite the poor visibility, I did the best I could when swinging my sword at its side as it came closer. Much of the mud around the surrounding tunnels had completely caved in.

I got a few swings in, each stab causing it to retreat backward. The deep tears were starting to anger the mutant more and it charged forward when I had stopped for a brief pause in between my careful attacks. There was just enough room near the entrance to a different tunnel to avoid the foul-smelling worm.

Castin started shooting at it with his submachine gun. I was certain he'd run out of bullets soon. The damage we were inflicting had punctured the creature's outer membrane and what turned out to be its vital organs. I continued thrashing at it harshly.

Adrenaline surged through me as I realized we were actually going to make it out alive. It was beginning to lose momentum and strength. I stood tiredly in the muddy tunnel, glad to have survived the short, yet frightening challenge. Eventually, the leech lay lifeless in the mud, its limp body falling back down where it came from in the deep mess.

"Are you both alright?" I asked as it grew quiet.

"I always am," Castin grunted from the corner.

Theo was quick to answer, "Yeah. I'm fine. Thank you for taking care of it. I would've never survived alone down here. Let's keep going, I'm sure we'll find my people soon."

"We're also looking for someone," I said as we continued onward. "I'm going to help save her life."

I got no response, as if the other two were doubtful that we all would be reunited.

As we progressed further, I realized that the middle tunnel had led us to a new type of fork in the road. The left and right tunnels were on either side of us, and each was flanked by four extra entryways.

"We should probably avoid the right side," I suggested. "It will eventually lead to the library's plumbing. That's what I saw on the map. It had the same layout as one of the schematics I looked at when searching for swords. So, we're heading left then."

Castin sounded exhausted, but managed to ask, "Do either of you want to use one of my guns? I have a few extra. I hardly have enough ammo for myself, to be honest, but figured I might as well ask you both."

"No thank you. I'd rather not get interrogated by anyone from the Frontier after this rescue," I replied.

"Same here. I know enough—trust me," Theo said, confusing us both, but we decided not to press the issue.

I was the first to go through the wide tunnel on the left side. It initially seemed to be the least narrow of them all, but after a few minutes, the space became more cramped which forced us to bend our knees and hunch our backs until we had no choice but to crawl to keep moving. I did the best I could to remain calm. *Inhale. Exhale. Slowly. Repeat.* I often reminded myself.

Theo broke what had become an uncomfortable and tense silence. "Not sure how much farther we can go. It's closing in a lot up here. We may have to turn around and try a different tunnel."

It had become entirely dark, and I struggled against rising claustrophobia as I barely managed to move. "I'm afraid that may not be an option now."

The sounds of our feet shuffling were drowning out the echoing taps of dripping water. Trying to move backward caused more dirt to fall and fill in where we'd just arrived from. Our exit was completely blocked. I held my breath momentarily as the passageway continued to narrow out, sometimes feeling something moving in the mud near my limbs.

It took probably around five minutes for us to reach the next entrance, which was the largest tunnel we'd been in. I made it through first, followed by Castin, and then Theo. I finally took desperate, deep breaths of somewhat fresher air when I was able to. Thankful for stretching and my blood flow returning to normal.

"Do you see that? Over there? Look!" I ran to the far-right side. "There's a hole with some light coming through! We might be closer to the surface than we think."

"Able to see anything on the other side?" Castin inquired.

"Not... really... actually, yeah. There seems to be a room in the distance with air flowing. That'll be our best bet at going forward. I'm not sure exactly where we are based on the schematics I've studied, but we shouldn't go right. That would lead us to the faulty plumbing system." I recalled the map in my mind.

"But why? What do you know about it that's keeping us from going that way? Sure, it's riskier than traveling under the library's storage rooms, but we might find life that way," Castin said, examining my discovery as he pushed aside a handful of mud to reveal more.

"Be careful. Messing with even a small part of this could cause the entire thing to collapse." I warned him. "The plumbing had a lot to do with Salt Crest City becoming what it is. It's not just the excessive water I'm worried about, but the chemical contents of it as well. We might escape the poison in the sky, but I think everyone here already knows that the water could threaten our chances of survival just as much."

Castin peered through the small sliver of light. "We won't drink it then. How about writing a command for some food and drinks? I'm dehydrated and starving."

"We have to be cautious about even touching the water," I replied. "We need to use our resources wisely and only when necessary. We might be close to finding Theia and the other lost group. If we withdraw this health restoration and something goes wrong, it won't be the best idea. Let's hold off on food and water while we check the left tunnel."

"I think we should go right and request those instead," Castin countered. "We need the nutrition and sustenance to make it through."

Theo stayed out of the argument, unsure of which side to take.

"Why abandon our unlimited supply of health vials for a meal? We should fast the hours out," I argued.

"Wouldn't that command be able to treat our symptoms of hunger and thirst?" Castin asked me.

"It doesn't work that way. Magic has specific rules. It handles those needs with different options and restorative properties." I barely had time to delve into all the details of countless manuscripts.

"Let's go left, then," Theo said. "If we're able to find that room on the other side, we'll probably be alright."

We were able to venture through the left tunnel comfortably, as the space allowed us to walk fully upright with our weapons at our sides.

As it finally grew easier to see, I also heard water falling as echoes of our footsteps magnified in depth. The mud underfoot felt like concrete, its color the only thing that hadn't changed. Shocks of pain ran up my achy legs from the hardened surface. The tunnel grew much colder as pieces of metal were exposed behind crumbled parts of its walls. I passed several clusters of bubbly holes that allowed light in. The air smelled of wet soil, and it only grew stronger as the next passageway came into view.

Light greeted us as we walked into it, relieved at the clear view of our surroundings for the first time in hours. The mud tunnels transitioned into metal, and at the breakaway points where they met, worms, mucus, and green sludge oozed from in between each side. I almost lost my footing with how slippery the ground was.

Something had fallen to our level and was moving towards us. Droplets cascaded as a loud thump accompanied the unsettling sounds.

"Get your weapons ready," Castin instructed.

"You may not need them," Theo added.

I watched the dimly lit hallway up ahead as a shower of droplets rained down from the ceiling. I kept my sword ready as someone stepped out from the shadows.

Castin looked down at his snowy mountain tattoo with a sour look. "Can't be the crew they said got 'relocated'…" He reloaded his gun.

"Theo! You made it back!" a woman in a camouflage hazmat suit emerged and hugged Theo warmly. "We tried looking everywhere for you! You must go find the others at once, they need you for the Euphrasia gate project!" Theo nodded into her shoulder, gave us a tearful look, and mouthed 'thank you' before quietly leaving. The woman carried a sword almost identical to mine. "My name is Krista. Who exactly are you both?"

"Most others call me the Librarian. I'm from Salt Crest City. I have no allegiance to the Frontier, though, I try to make that as clear as possible." I stood taller.

Castin extended his arms to bring attention to his tattoos. "*I* am associated with the Frontier. I'm sure you've already guessed that but figured I'd let you know upfront. You'd have seen my tatts sooner or later. My name is Castin."

"State your department," Krista said coldly while looking at his guns with skepticism and judgment.

He waved his pistol around with a bout of forced laughter. "Uh, what do you think? Do you really need my title and subdivision? I'm a well-trained chief officer within the Emergency Biohazard division. I oversee toxic chemical cleanup, since you must know."

She accepted his answer with a shrug. "You both may proceed through the next tunnel with me. We actually need your help to break a toxic barrier a few miles south. The Forgotten, that's us down here, found an exit. It's not far from where we are now. We'll have to go through the underground library."

"We could use your help too. We're searching for a missing person and haven't been able to find her anywhere," I chimed in, trying to keep my tone uplifting with my next words. "But I believe she'll make it back unscathed, even though it feels like trying to find a needle in a haystack. I won't lose hope."

TULE

Morning

CHAPTER EIGHT: EYEBRIGHT

IT WAS EARLY MORNING WHEN THE NEWS
broke that Theia was missing and two of our own had
gone down into the tunnels to save her. I had no idea
what events led to her sudden disappearance, and
neither did Zekiel, despite being close to the accident
right before it happened. *I hope they are okay down
there... It's so unsafe.* I trusted him, though, when he
said he didn't know what caused the disaster. Hours
were slipping away, as I believed the storm would be

starting within the next day. Even though time wasn't on my side, I was determined to not lose hope that things would somehow work out for us.

Mud bubbles appeared more frequently and grew larger, a sign that hidden experiments would soon crawl out of them. We all eventually called them sells. Their odd and terrifying characteristics made them hard to forget. These creatures could survive both on land and in the ocean. They resembled overgrown salamanders with extra legs, combined with jellyfish-like tentacles, venomous and swaying as they moved. Most were medium-sized, just tall enough to reach past our knees.

Their joints clicked loudly—probably from dehydration and fatigue. The older they were, the faster they moved. Sells would sometimes leave us alone if unprovoked, but something had set them off today. Many thought it was the noise from the armory, where survivors had been crafting and altering outfits for hours.

It was early morning when a pack of mutants traveled towards the gates, clawing away at the foundation. A group of four gray-clad marksmen with sniper rifles held the sells at bay for a while, but luck was running out as they multiplied.

"Getting low on ammo!" one of them yelled, his voice tense.

"Don't worry!" another marksman called out, peering over the ledge. "They can't get up here!"

He'd spoken too soon. The sells began climbing on top of each other, steadily reaching the entrance.

"Those things will be up here in no time, and… a-and they—look!" he yelled, pointing at the gates.

One of the creatures had managed to climb higher than the others and jumped through the gate. Its swinging tentacles thumped against the iron poles as it passed between them, heading towards the survivors—two dressed in gray, the other in purple. Someone stepped forward to defend them, firing a small pistol but missing each shot.

"Do you even know how to aim?" a woman in gray asked judgmentally, yanking the gun from her hands.

But before she could react further, the sell was airborne, hurling itself toward her. It landed against her block, its legs thrashing against her armored elbows.

"Get it off!" she screamed desperately, dropping her gun in the struggle.

The weapon slid across the ground, its polished metal scraping loudly as it stopped at the feet of the person in purple. "If what they say is true, is it worth switching sides?" the citygoer muttered, almost to themselves.

Meanwhile, the sell's tentacles lashed across the woman's face, tearing flesh from her cheeks as they stung her. Blood streamed into her eyes as she fought to free herself. I winced and looked away at the sight.

I hope she will be able to recover from this attack.

Another man in purple grabbed the gun before she could reach it. "Never hesitate!" he shouted, pulling the trigger. The others watched in stunned silence as the creature fell after his choice of changing sides to help.

What else could be lurking in the tunnels? I wondered. So many things remained hidden, just as other life forms and magical secrets lay concealed in the darkness. *I hope that everyone down there comes back safely.*

By midday, I decided to visit Crow Library to see if I could find anything that might help us. Foreboding, dust-covered statues stood in front of the abandoned building. The one positioned furthest in the front was a large, broken crow, its beak still pointy and its eyes hollow after someone had smashed them out. Tattered flags hung from wooden railroad beams on either side of the entrance. The lavender tones of the fabric had begun to fade, and whatever text had once been there was now unreadable.

Each heavy iron handle was intricately handcrafted, shaped into woven vines in the same gunmetal shade that covered half the floors. A checkered print of gray and white spread across each room, barely visible beneath heaps of dust.

At the front stood a secretary's desk, strewn with old invoices, overdue stamps, and folders labeled 'Fines', 'Agreements', and 'Bibliographic Records'. I leafed through a few, spotting black-and-white headshots of various people. Some faces showed worry, others were entirely emotionless.

I found a reminder that there were files from prior to when I began going by my family's last name, Tule, instead of my first one after they finally adopted me:

AVANA TULE

Every header was stamped with 'The Frontier'. The personal information section of my file was mostly obscured by a rather large note, which I peeled back to reveal a warning and sequence of digits I recognized:

CONFIDENTIAL
F.E.M. #345

I glanced up at the library's interior, taking in a blue banner that connected the historical and fictional sections. It read: 'You can't have one without the other'. My eyes wandered until I noticed an old radio transmitter. I fiddled with the dial, tuning through several frequencies before catching a man's robotic voice sharing terrible news, yet devoid of emotion,

"How long has it been since they've started rising? That wasn't an earthquake earlier. The magnetic countdown is going into full effect. You know, th–"

Static overtook his next words to who was presumably another researcher. My heart raced as I twisted the dial again, trying to catch more of his message. *Is what he's saying true!?* Most of my concerns were occupied by the upcoming storm, those down in the tunnels, and the terrifying creatures that threatened our safety. But this had raised the stakes higher than I could have imagined. *This is F.E.M.!*

I frantically searched the unfamiliar sections of the library, skimming through the pages of books I had been saving to read later, hoping to find a remedy or a clearer clue about what to do next.

It was still very dark outside despite it being a hot morning. There were thankfully candles that I could light to see the seldom-read paragraphs better. *I wonder how many people have taken the time to study these? Am I one of just a few who even looks in here at all? If only I could speak with another avid reader. It would be nice to have deeper discussions about all of this.*

Time slipped by, and no matter how long I waited, I didn't hear the voices on the radio again. *There has to be something here.* Eventually, I reached a set of books written by the anonymous author I had once told Zekiel about. *Wait!* Out of many books, there was one that was a cloudy green. It stood out more than the rest at a first glance, and I figured there had to be something useful to learn inside.

It was the dustiest book in the series, and its table of contents listed topics that eerily paralleled the problems we were facing. I jotted down a couple notes, then returned to my room. *I really need to unwind.*

As I sprawled the marked pages across my mattress, I lit a joint, smoking them always eased my nerves. Through the window, the ocean lay still, a false sense of peace in contrast to the storm looming outside. My room was dim, the only brightness from the candles.

A sudden knock at the door broke the quiet.

I knew who it was.

"Hey, is it okay if I come in?" Zekiel's voice sounded deeper than usual from outside.

"Of course," I replied, I wanted nothing more than to talk about the current events before things worsened. "I was hoping to talk to you about everything that's been going on while we still have a chance to."

As he entered, I was shocked by the sight of the rare sword Elijah had once carried, which he rested against the nearest wall. "He gave this to me earlier," Zekiel said, shrugging. "Told me I could keep it."

"Really? That's so nice of him." I couldn't help but admire the weapon. Its craftsmanship was breathtaking, and its purposeful design was one of the coolest I'd ever seen. *I would love to add that to my personal collection.*

"Yeah," he agreed, following me into the room. "He can be alright sometimes. How've you been holding up?"

"Doing my best to stay calm," I said, tidying the space as much as possible. He had only been in my kitchen and living room before. "You?"

"I'm dealing with this much better than the old me would have, that's for sure," he admitted, laughing—a sound that made me smile wider than I expected.

We shared a long, comforting hug before I closed the door behind us.

Zekiel sat onto the nearest chair. "Have you seen those creatures attacking the city lately? Those things I've helped Ezra and Castin defeat. Others refer to them as... lizards?"

"I wouldn't exactly call them that," I said, sitting across from him. "Sells live near the water, sometimes above it, and they travel in packs. It's unsettling seeing them even from miles away. I haven't observed them up close, though. And honestly? I hope it stays that way. Within the gates, we should be safe. I'm glad that you three made it back okay. The real challenge is getting everyone else to cooperate."

"Is anything else going on?"

"Yeah, we may somehow have an even bigger problem," I paused, hesitating before continuing. "I overheard some of the Frontier members talking over a frequency in the library. Apparently, some sort of 'magnetic force' is pulling us upwards now. I haven't felt anything, though. Have you?"

"I can't believe you just said that so casually," he replied, smirking, though I could see the worry lurking behind his eyes. "I haven't felt anything either. Hopefully, it's just fake news. Some of your coworkers seem like the type who would create cover-ups, going so far as to lie to distract us."

How does he know? I frowned, then responded, "I try my best to spread the truth and make sure I do my research first. Thank you for understanding how my work is. I tend to get buried in it, as you can tell. It means a lot that you've done everything possible to help me so far with this. I admire how brave you are."

"Thank you, but if you knew me before, you wouldn't be saying that," he muttered, then added more loudly, "My memories... I can't go back to that way of living. I want nothing to do with anyone or anything that reminds me of where I came from. The woods. I won't venture back into them when I have a compass guiding me away from my past."

"You were given another chance," I said.

"Yeah," he agreed, his voice tinged with emotion. "I had an epiphany when I arrived here. I was excited about the future and overwhelmed by the opportunities. I tried to abandon myself. In fact, that's what I used to want more than anything—just to float in nothingness. But I was wrong. I didn't know what was best back then."

"How do you feel now?" I asked after a few moments.

"Better," Zekiel said, but then he abruptly looked away. "Thank you for believing in me, but I have to go."

"Why? Is everything okay?" I asked, concern flooding my voice as he hurriedly got up from his chair. I could tell that he had a lot on his mind.

Is there something he's not telling me? I searched his face for an answer.

"No," he replied, avoiding eye contact. "I just need to take a walk and clear my head. I'll talk to you later." He let his hair fall over his face as he moved to leave.

But I didn't let him go like that. I followed him outside, where others gave us judgmental glances, recognized from playing my tapes at Sea Bartering.

"We can talk later, Tule," he said. "I'm fine. I just need some space, that's all."

"I sense that something else is going on," I pressed. "Do you want to talk about it? I don't want anything bad to happen to you, or for you to... hurt yourself in some way."

He hesitated, his silence worried me, before finally speaking. "I'm not going to."

"If you need space, I understand," I said patiently. "But just know, with whatever is going on in your head, you're never alone. We can be friends here."

Zekiel remained quiet, as he usually did.

The changes in the sky were impossible to ignore. Electric currents streaked above us, small lines of neon dissecting the darkness as forest-green smoke seeped out. Some witnessing the event had been anticipating its arrival for several days. *Why didn't more of the others believe me?* I thought about the shop visitors who hadn't listened to my warnings. *Maybe I need to be more succinct?*

Panic was setting in as survivors rubbed their eyes, which had become red and swollen from the poisonous particles in the air. Many were asking, "What do we do?" and "What is this?!"

A few people shot me dirty looks. I kept my hood up as I ushered some of the frightened onlookers inside. Zekiel was close by, watching the mist, his expression was concerned as the threat unfolded. He closed the storage room door as we waited out the fifteen-minute-long storm. I kept repeating that I didn't know how to help those who needed care.

They will feel better once the storm subsides, right?

I was wrong.

Even after the green cracks in the sky disappeared, the effects lingered on the citygoers.

If this is what's happening up here... then what's going on down below?

It took about thirty minutes for the air to become breathable again. Many fled outdoors as soon as they could, the heat inside magnified by poor ventilation. Even after the storm subsided, particulate matter floated through the air.

I recalled what I had read about earlier, my mind wandering to the garden that I often tended to. *That flower from the preface...* I snapped my fingers, watching the mist swirl. *What if we have it? It's worth checking. Who knows when the poison will return?*

Panic was at an all-time high, but I decided to head to the garden once things calmed down. I remembered descriptions of a plant capable of healing infectious eye diseases—white, yellow, and purple petals. *I know we have these! One of my favorites.*

Inside the secluded greenhouse, I marveled at the array of plants. The air was warm and sweet, unlike the harsh odors outside. The scent of cinnamon soil greeted me as I stepped in. I touched the soft, sturdy stems that held them upright. *It's impressive how they've managed to stay alive through all of this.* Then, I spotted a patch of eyebright flowers. *How much water do they need?* I clutched my stomach and tried to ignore the symptoms of dehydration. *Probably more than I have been getting.*

I crouched closer to the special flowers and began plucking them one by one, carefully removing each from the soil they were used to living in; where they had bloomed. *I've heard that speaking kindly to plants helps them grow.*

"Sorry I'm taking you out of your comfort zone," I whispered.

The leaves had a distinct curvature, with a drop of orange pigment in the middle of the white petals, and streaks of purple lining the underside. As I collected them, I noticed a mini notebook I had accidentally left behind earlier. On the cover was a single word:

EUPHRASIA

"We need antibiotics," I told the flowers as I tied the stems together, weaving them into a strong core until they formed a ball. I took a step back, raised my hand in their direction, and asked, "Can you come over here?"

The flowers began slowly rolling towards me.

Excited, I found Zekiel near the training arena and rushed to tell him about what I'd put together. "This is a healing companion. For when the poison returns," I explained as we headed back to the greenhouse.

It was by luck that I had managed to get some of the help we needed just in time. A few hours later, another storm hit, worse than the last. The sky looked like shattered green glass, and smoke leaked through the cracks. People scrambled to find shelter as their eyes burned from the poison.

I could hardly see as the others fled inside again to be shielded from the mist. A few dressed in gray went around the perimeter and secured all of the windows with the help of ladders. The fifteen-minute-long ordeal was going to wreak more havoc than the last one, the sky greener and the poison stronger and most likely lethal.

Zekiel had been outside with me when the storm started. The garden I tended was destroyed as the plastic walls around it melted, along with the pots that housed my plants. *I've lost my safe place. My only home here.* Unfortunately, most of the marijuana was completely gone. I fought back tears at what was lost.

The part of Salt Crest City that had brought peace, life, and a sense of home was decimated.

The only thing that survived were the eyebright flowers. I had always given them special care because my mother used to grow them. To my surprise, the floral companion I had created rolled through the chaos, offering relief to those close enough to benefit from it. Eyebright's center released a fog that soothed and healed the burning eyes of the survivors.

That medicinal mist only reached those close enough—but it also triggered rain to fall at the same time. The droplets consisted of water mixed with chemical compounds similar to those found in eye drops. Survivors who needed relief stood outside and opened their eyes wider to let it wash them once a few discovered what was happening before they reached cover.

Despite Zekiel's initial strong desire to leave any sort of magic behind when I first met him, I could sense both his relief at the restorative events unfolding and a deep sense of what seemed to be wonder.

"It's helping!" Ezra called out to the others, who were still covering their eyes and pushing past each other to get inside. "Let the drops in!"

A few glanced his way, seeing the relief in his expression, and followed his lead. I looked down at Eyebright, now sitting at my feet with slightly bruised petals. People raised their arms to the sky in excitement as they were cured.

But the relief was short-lived. Once the storm subsided, a new disaster took its place. The mud beneath us began to cave in from the center, creating a vortex as another cloudy storm was approaching on the horizon.

The force of our foundation breaking wasn't pulling us downwards. Instead, we began to rise. Every hour, more mud fell into what resembled a sinkhole as it filled up with the ocean's untouched waters. We were moving towards the worsening poison.

The eyebright flower had been a temporary cure for a much bigger problem.

We needed to leave the city, but jumping down was not an option. Many were against trying to survive that way, especially after Theia disappeared. Teleportation was the only viable possibility to get everyone to safer ground, as the mud was nearly impossible to walk on. *When will we ever see Theia, Castin, and whoever else is down in the tunnels again? I need to know that they're okay!*

We were critically low on water, leaving many survivors desperately dehydrated, and the hot air made it even harder to endure.

Everyone armed themselves. About half of the city's members wore purple, slightly less than half were in gray, and a small percentage were dressed entirely in black. Elijah was proudly part of that minimal group. Some claimed they wore colorful attire only because of the heat. Several questioned the need to pick sides, but it turned out that options were limited due to the scarcity of clothing. Those still wearing their arrival outfits eventually changed, as the weather dirtied their clothes or they had to cover up with mismatched armor pieces.

Elijah had been running around more than anyone else, frantically searching for something. He had combed through every inch of the five main buildings and their supporting quarters. At one point, his lap turned into a sprint as he chased a crew member from the Emergency Biohazard team who was carrying something in his hands.

"Don't get rid of it!" Elijah called out, breathless. "It has nothing to do with magic, I swear! It's just regular armor! I was holding onto it for someone else and covered it up to protect it!"

The item was suddenly thrown over the gate. "We take things that are related to curses very seriously here," came the response.

"No!" Elijah shouted, rushing to the edge. "Why'd you do that?"

"I'll help you get whatever that was!" I offered, stepping forward. *Must be important.* "The sound has already attracted sells!"

"Alright, thanks!" Elijah said, nodding. "Let's go before it's torn up!"

Zekiel, who seemed a bit tense as he drew his new sword, joined us. Elijah dashed ahead, leaping into the mud and splattering it onto his black pants.

The mutants, with their many feet and venomous tentacles sprouting from rough skin, moved in various directions. They secreted venom from giant parasitic pores. Some had fallen into sinkholes, making us city dwellers grateful for the unpredictability of the ruins.

Growling sells were quickly making their way to the package, and one had already grabbed it before Elijah could reach it. It ran off before any of us could catch up.

"No!" He yelled out in despair, then turned to fight off the sells that were close to nipping his heels.

Incendiary rounds fired from the guns of those inside the gate struck a handful of them. Three were engulfed in flames, while the others only faced a brief flicker of fire. They screeched in response and ran even faster.

Elijah joined Zekiel and me in attacking the creatures with his sword as another pack was alerted by the noise. Over ten more were approaching. The hot raindrops caused blisters on my skin and made my eyes sting. A few fighters in gray took down most of the mutants with their SMGs. One by one, they fell as their flesh was torn apart by bullets and blades.

The sells tried to bite through our armor, but the combat leather and bulletproof metal held strong.

Their thumping footsteps rushed towards the city, accompanied by hungry growls. The venom from the recent storm had made them even more dangerous, causing further mutations. Heaps of mud splashed around them as they advanced.

More packs were heading our way.

"They're going to climb on top of each other to get up here again!" the others yelled down to Elijah, Zekiel, and me.

With no choice but to stay on the ground to fend off the attack, we continued brutally fighting all of them with our swords as everyone else was rising above us.

The city would soon be out of reach.

THE LIBRARIAN

Afternoon-Evening

CHAPTER NINE: TUNNEL MAZE

I SILENTLY HOPED, WITH EACH PASSING second, that the woman we met, Krista, would lead us to Theia. She had found Castin and me wandering in one of the tunnels and asked for our help in opening a door stuck with a 'toxic barrier'. We hadn't yet seen what she was referring to but followed her as she led us to others who had apparently been left behind by the Frontier. I kept my book in hand, thankful it had healing capabilities, but worried luck might run out.

"Do you have any health kits?" I asked Krista.

She replied with certainty, "We have plenty." Her answer didn't put me at ease, though.

"You called yourself part of 'the Forgotten'. I think I know which crew you belonged to," Castin said with a sad expression. "What did they leave you with?"

She continued leading the way as her pace quickened. "You'll see. A whole lot of mismatched components, which was intentional, of course. We weren't given the tools to survive on our own, but Old Crow Library will have what we need. They didn't think we'd ever get into it." Krista glanced back at Castin's guns. I could hardly see her face due to her full-body suit, but I imagined it was full of annoyance. "By the way, there'll be no need for any of those here."

"I'll be the judge of that." He kept his hands pried onto them. "Last thing I'm doing is giving these up."

I redirected the conversation once they each grew silent, "Krista, does your group have food or drinks?"

"Yes, the higher-ups left plenty of packaged goods before they sent us to rot in our premature graves."

The wide tunnel was covered in graffiti, and echoes trailed back to where we'd just been. Castin ran his hands along it with a sentimental smile as if he was the one who'd painted them. "The Drifters left this here."

I had never met one before but heard a lot about them. They were one massive gang who were known for causing chaos and corrupting F.E.M. on insane levels. "They unloaded half of their paint cans on the ruins before the Frontier took it from them. I've read about what happened. The reason they even came down into these tunnels at all was to run from the law."

"That *isn't* possible." Castin shook his head. "The Emergency Biohazard crew was the first to the city. I wouldn't be surprised if some detectives may have written faulty records in that library. There were several others occupying the space of us from either side of the Frontier who were brought to carry out..."

Krista shot him a tense look before glancing at me. He continued, "...what we had to do."

"Got it." *I can find out more about the city's origins later, I know the records I've read aren't faulty, I think Castin might be though. He has nothing to gain by being truthful it seems.* The tunnel stretched on for a few more miles, the longest we'd ventured through. "Krista, I have a question, your health kits—what can they restore? I have something called a F.E.M.Book, and I can command potions that could heal anything."

"Oh. *Really?*" Her steps slowed while leading the way. "Please don't mention that around anyone else. It could put you in danger. If any of us get injured then we need to use one of my department-approved health kits."

Those won't be able to help as much as the F.E.M.Book can. I inhaled deeply. "I understand that sometimes magic should remain hidden." *But we need to lay low.*

"Exactly." Krista seemed to sigh in relief at my response.

Castin jumped in, "Sometimes we need it to save us."

"I think we should follow suggestions for now. We should be fine not casting any spells from it for a little while. Hopefully, we won't need to before finding Theia." I made sure all of my pockets were zipped up. "At least it's holding onto the health vial selection. I don't want to switch it to something else. It's better to have this power activated in case of an emergency."

"The hideout is just up ahead," Krista said.

As we approached a hut made of metal sheets towards the back right of the tunnel, our sources of light began to diminish. The walls had fewer holes letting in any rays, and for the first time, we saw flickering candles in the maze of mud.

"It's getting colder the further down we go," I remarked.

"Can't help with that," Krista said, sliding one of the sheets to the side. "But at least we have enough food and water for everyone."

Behind the divider was a cramped room with many items covered, sealed, and wrapped in dirty plastic. Lanterns in each corner cast a warm glow over the dreary space. Three others in matching hazmat suits were either leaning against the walls or sitting on a duct-tape-covered air mattress.

We had just walked in on their conversation.

"I think that's the most ridiculous thing about it all, you know? Like... how are you going to spend *that* much money on resources just to create fake vaults?" one of them said.

"I heard it was always a part of their plan. Got people talking, didn't it? Got their attention directed on the wrong thing. How many sad suckers fell for it? Who believes that they'd actually put them there for everyone to see?" another responded.

Krista cleared her throat. "I'm back. With company."

"We can see that." One of the men stood up from the ground to face us. "How are these guys even breathing? Got any Geiger counters? You may have underlying health issues that you aren't aware of yet."

"Please feel free to take what you need." Krista gestured toward their crates of food and bottled water. "Unfortunately, we don't have extra suits."

Castin and I ate and drank ravenously, hardly pausing between bites and sips as we tore open package sleeves and held onto fistfuls of bottle caps.

"So, why are you down here?" the researcher leaning against the wall inquired.

"A woman—Theia—disappeared. She fell through part of the mud that caved in," Castin explained and then promptly turned to ask me without a second thought, "Can that book craft us clothes?"

"What sort of 'book' are you talking about?" The third person in a suit looked at Krista. "You didn't bring Magic Wielders here, did you?"

I adjusted my glasses. "Wait. Let's ta—"

"What are you going to do about it anyway?" Castin hastily pulled out his SMG.

"Woah! Put that away!" one of the strangers exclaimed.

The others spoke in angry, threatening tones. "You're not allowed to use that here!"

The three in camouflage drew their swords.

Castin rolled his shoulders and let out an impatient sigh. "I was told by Krista here that you need help getting through some sort of barrier—a toxic entrance to the underground portion, right? Of Old Crow?"

The trio nodded, their names hidden on the backs of their clothing, yet they kept their guards up at us.

"Well then, you're going to let me do things *my* way." Castin pointed his gun at Krista. "Tell 'em."

One of the others pressed the tip of his sword against Castin's back, leaving an indent in the gray leather. "Put that down, now, try hard. Do you even realize you're aiming a gun at Euphrasia Arms' boss?"

"Thank you," Krista spoke with relief as Castin lowered his weapon and then nodded for the others to speak. "Please introduce yourselves, names only."

"Trav," the tallest stated.

"Abela," the person to his left answered.

The third Forgotten's suit was the most damaged of the three. "You can call me Cam."

"The four of us need help breaking through some sort of substance that's clinging to the door frame near our left. If the schematics we've reviewed are correct, it will lead us to the library's attic." Krista took her time to explain. "We can work our way through it, not only to look for Theia but also to find the basement exit."

"Thanks for explaining. I agree that Castin should take a look at it," I said, not wanting to get too involved. *I'll help when needed but will also still lay low.*

Krista nodded at Castin who was nearby. "I give you permission to use your gun over there if you see fit. Just don't point it at any of us again. Alright?"

He motioned to the mountains inked on his arm. "I don't answer to you, but thanks for your permission. Librarian, can we talk for a quick sec before I check?"

"Sure thing." I didn't speak again until we'd left.

We stepped away from the metal shack to speak privately. Castin checked his gun and ammo inventory. "Got any other books? A notebook will suffice."

"Yeah." I paused before reviewing my current inventory, eager to understand why he was asking for one. "Is that really what you want to talk about?"

He looked around to make sure we weren't being listened to before responding and avoiding eye contact. "Yep, and I need a pen. How much will this cost?"

"Twenty-five bay dollars, but why even pay me? No point down here anyways." I handed him a notebook and a ballpoint pen from one of my many pockets. "There you go. Just take them for free."

"No. I don't accept handouts, and I pay small business owners what they are owed. I respect the hustle, even if it's pushing black market products." Castin waved his hands at me to refuse the help.

Did I just hear him correctly? "You've never bought from me before. How would you know what I sell? Not that I'm... confirming." *I don't want him to report me.*

"Don't think I haven't met any of your buyers? Some are my friends." Castin nodded and handed me a handful of screws. "Here's the total. Keep the change."

"Are you both almost done?" Krista stepped over to us. "We're wasting a lot of time."

Castin held his submachine gun up, his finger hovering near the chrome trigger, as he walked past me. "On my way right now to check it out."

After grabbing one of the lanterns, he went over to see what the others were referring to. The thick silver door was covered sin green mush, dripping off the frame and sliding down either side. The rest of us moved as close as we could to watch.

The door was unlocked and only partially open, with a line of darkness visible to the left. Sludge covered most of the hinged metal, including the rusty handle and the floor underneath. The concrete was slippery under Castin's feet as he held the lantern closer. The increasing warmth caused the unknown substance to fall more slowly, its consistency becoming thicker from the heat. He used his free hand to touch some of it, allowing it to make direct contact with his finger.

"Are you okay?" I was the only one to ask.

Castin used his gun to shoot through the sludge, breaking the barrier to the other side. "We all will be."

He used the same hand to push the door all the way open, the residue sticking like adhesive but seeming to cause no damage. "This is nothing more than jellified remnants of a medicinal mist. It even smells like flowers."

"Our blades weren't strong enough to cut through it," Krista said, looking at her sword and then at the entrance.

The suited Forgotten crew stood in disbelief at Castin's discovery. He had already passed through the doorway before anything else was said. We followed, each holding lanterns, and I felt great anticipation about the secrets we might uncover.

One by one, we entered the dirty attic of what was called Old Crow Library, a hidden location that resembled the one above. It was filled with dust and storage boxes, held closed with pieces of duct tape, and marked with cryptic words written in black ink:

DON'T OPEN

CAUTION

WILL DETONATE

"Everyone, please be careful around these boxes, alright?" When I noticed the last one, I spoke up in between coughs. Then I could've sworn that I heard a faint sound of someone yelling somewhere in the distance. "Hold on. Did anyone else just hear that?"

We held our breaths, waiting in silence for—

One. Two. Three. F—

A muffled voice shouted, "Here! I am down here!"

"Someone's on the level below! Let's go check! It could be Theia!" I said urgently, drawing my sword and carefully stepping past many stacks of boxes.

We maneuvered through the cluttered space, the abandoned storage causing dust to billow with each step. My throat felt scratchy, and I could see that Castin, without a suit, was struggling even more.

"Hey... you need to please craft an item!" Castin managed to say through his coughing fit, his breathing became labored as he grabbed at his neck in distress.

I quickly dipped my feather into the whimsical ink and wrote on the next page, as the previous ones had been damaged. With that, I undid our health potion.

F.E.M.: HazardMask (2)

Two masks appeared, falling from a hole in the back cover, wrapped in contaminant-free packaging. Castin and I donned the white coverings, finally able to breathe properly. Moments later, we reached the voice on the level from underneath where we were and discovered who was calling out to us.

Tears welled up in my eyes as I saw Theia trapped under the rubble where she had gotten stuck.

"Here!" Theia's voice cried out.

Running over, it didn't take long to see that she was in critical condition.

Dying from injuries a department kit couldn't fix. She needed a F.E.M.Book health potion.

I began to clear some of the broken items away. The fourth story we were on was surprisingly spacious despite the destruction and collapse. The lower levels were filled with more manuscripts, reminding me of those up above trying to survive. I wasn't sure of their condition, how much time was left, or much else. Everything felt out of my control, yet I remained calm.

"I'm sorry it took me forever to get here," I said.

"Please don't apologize... I'm just glad *you* are okay. I've been here for what feels like a few hours," Theia replied, her voice weak. Her armor was covered in dust, and the black leather flaps were coated with debris. Her exposed skin was scratched up. "I've been getting colder, no water, and my nerves are acting up."

"When did the issues start?" I asked, throwing aside another rock as the others began helping.

"A while ago. It's a really long story," she sighed.

Theia's legs were pinned, leaving her torso mostly free. Her blood flow was being restricted by the wreckage. I hoped she'd be okay. We took turns removing the rubble more quickly as our muscles grew tired. I used my sword to push away the remaining ruins, finally freeing her after several desperate minutes. *I hope that everyone else is okay, too. Those that know the truth... they can't be lost.*

Theia's eyes lit up with relief when she saw me as she was finally freed from the checkered flooring, and held out her hand. "You really came down here to save me?"

"Yeah," I said, crouching down and taking her hand in mine.

"I'm glad it's you. I really need your help," she winced. "It feels like pins and needles are jamming into my stomach. I could be bleeding internally. Something might have ruptured. May you please use that book of yours to help me?"

I frowned behind my face mask, my chest tightening. "I'm afraid I can't. I'm so sorry."

"There's only one other option now: the armor I'm wearing. Magic Wielders are granted one type of ability from it. It won't help in this case if I activate mine, though," Theia said, facing me. "But *you* haven't tried it."

"Why me? I'm not a–"

"Magic Wielder. I already know that you are," she interrupted. "I'm not worried about your past; what matters is right here and now. Okay? I'll keep you safe with this information getting out. I promise."

I took my glasses off and covered my face. *I can't discuss this with anyone else right now. There's so much they don't need to know about me, that other friends don't even know. Will I ever see them again and tell them everything? I can't have the law capture me before then.*

My eyes were watery as I looked down at Theia who was barely clinging to life. "Okay. I'll put it on."

She asked for my help removing it, and after I was able to with no problems, she placed it in my hands. Theia seemed surprised by how effortlessly I'd taken the armor off of her, as if it brought her a great sense of relief. "Thank you for everything you've done. I knew you'd be able to assist me."

The four from the Experiment Sciences department stood stiffly by empty tables and chairs on either side of us, whispering to each other.

"We *need* to talk after this," Krista said harshly.

I nodded and then retreated behind one of the bookshelves for privacy, putting the leather armor on underneath my coat. Everyone else waited quietly for me to emerge. Theia could barely keep her eyes open with sluggish blinks, and her breathing was labored. I was incredibly nervous. The last thing I wanted to do was let anyone down. I took a few deep breaths before making my way over and kneeling beside her.

"I haven't tried this on anyone else before, but now's a good time," I said, resting a hand on her trembling shoulder. "Are you doing alright, Theia?"

"I-I'm not sure. No. I'm not, I'm not okay," she replied weakly.

"It's going to be okay. I'll do the best I can. I promise."

"I can't believe this is happening right now," Abela said in a judgmental tone to the other scientists.

I placed my hand near Theia's collarbone, and she put hers on the side of my sore arm, her touch offering a sense of friendly reassurance that all would be okay. We locked eyes, not breaking contact for a moment.

"Thank you for using your powers to help," she said, giving me a smile. "I'm not used to others harnessing it for good."

When I had met her outside the library on a cloudy night, I had no idea I would one day be saving her life. We had spent time together researching before, but never like this, not under life-or-death circumstances.

It hurt me deeply to see her so hopeless and in such suffering. I wanted to take her pain and endure it instead. *I wonder how her nerves are doing?* Every part of me wanted nothing more than to bring her healing. I steadily traced my fingertips along the top of her chest, down each of her arms, and brought them up and along the sides of her tear-streaked face.

"It's okay," I leaned in close so that only she could hear. "I will help you right now."

"I'm just really scared. I-I think I might be dying. I can't go like this—I can't. There's so much I haven't set right yet. I need more time to live." Her face was etched with despair as she struggled to speak.

Tiny yellow stars started to push out from the lines of my fingertips, shifting into rays of smoke that seeped into her pores. "I will help you," I repeated.

Theia reached up and took a handful of her long hair, tucking half of it behind an ear. "At least I get to have you here with me amidst all this."

"Yeah?" I focused on ensuring that the concoction continued to flow from me through concentration.

"Of course. By choosing to rescue me... you've already helped me feel something again when I wasn't sure that I ever would. I didn't think that I'd ever feel whole again after my injury, the love I lost, and who I became. You've reminded me of the good in humanity after living in darkness, sickness, and misery."

A few of my tears pooled on my glasses.

I had forgotten that everyone else was in the room as I placed both hands gently on either side of her head. Curative stars continued to pour out of me. "I'd do anything to help."

"I know and I can hardly believe it. I don't think that anyone else would've jumped in those tunnels to rescue me." Theia's eyes were wide with appreciation.

"Didn't you notice?" I asked, nodding towards Castin. "He joined in to help too."

Theia mouthed a silent thank you to Castin, who tried to shrug it off with a small wave. "Don't give me too much credit. Sure, I wanted you to be alright, but even if you had passed away quickly, I still had to go down to retrieve the armor you were wearing. It's something that could save everyone else. Don't take it personally."

We looked away from him as he seemed to be holding back tears, perhaps feeling more than he let on.

"Can you please tell me something?" I asked.

"Yeah," she replied, already sounding a bit stronger, which was more like herself.

I motioned toward her shaky index finger. "Is this where your damage is the worst?" After she nodded solemnly I leaned down, letting my hair obscure the view from everyone else, and held her hand as yellow rays of light flared brightly between us. She took a deep breath and sat up straighter at the contact.

Theia pulled me into a tight hug, getting my coat covered in grime. I'd never been happier to have it dirtied.

"How are you feeling?" I asked.

"Already so much better." She held me close. "Thank you."

"You're welcome." We stayed in that embrace for a moment longer.

"I'm going to be honest," Castin said next. "I didn't think we would find you, Theia. Not like this. You're tough to have survived what you did. That's how us Magic Wielders are, though."

She gave him a grateful smile. "I knew you had some good in you, Castin."

"Yeah, yeah, yeah. Whatever," he said, smiling back.

"Now we need to get through the rest of the library," Krista reminded us with a sharp look.

We cleared the fourth level, finding only abandoned stationery, tables, chairs, books, and a few trash cans. Most of the higher levels were archived storage, with a few bibliographic secrets hidden among the regular items. I recognized everything.

It was time to descend the first staircase. Each step was creaky and unsteady, the checkered-painted wood rotting away beneath our boots. Extra dust fell with our weight as we reached the third floor.

I recognized much of the architecture and the items; this library was designed to be nearly identical to the one on Salt Crest. The checkered floors were reversed, with gunmetal gray and white switched from their original positions. Although the literary texts initially appeared to mimic those from the city's original location, closer inspection revealed inconsistencies.

When we reached the next set of stairs, I saw a thin string at my feet just before the top step. "There are traps here. Be careful."

"I'll disarm it," Krista said, using her sword to cut down the trap. We kept a safe distance as it released a cloud of smoke with a loud boom. "I wonder what they used. It seems more smoke and mirrors than anything else. Still, be cautious; whoever set this up might be trying to catch us off guard."

"I can tell you who," Trav began. "The Drifters. This has their name written all over it, along with the graffiti on the walls. Of course, it's the degenerates."

Castin clenched his fists at the remark.

Abela scoffed and crossed her arms. "You're right. They made this place their campout."

Theia chimed in, "So we're intruders to them."

"Yes, but technically *they* are," Krista clarified. "They'll likely try to attack if they spot us before we manage to get out of here. Stay on high alert."

We scoped out the entire level in a matter of minutes, each of us taking a different path to ensure the coast was clear. During our search, we came upon a handful of other traps hidden in almost every corner. Dust plumed in the air, and Theia began coughing roughly into her arm.

"Here," Castin said, offering her his mask. "Take my gear. We don't have any other ones."

"What would you wear then?" she asked.

"Hm, I dunno, maybe steal some equipment off of Trav here," Castin replied with a dirty look in his direction. "Sounds like something a degenerate would do… right?"

"I don't know what your problem is, but keep it to yourself. Alright?" Trav said, visibly uncomfortable.

I walked over to Theia, moving away from the science fiction section. "You must've forgotten. I can craft spells infinitely until a change of command." I retrieved my book, feather, and ink, and wrote the phrase again in front of her:

F.E.M.: HazardMask (2)

I had to turn to a new page to reissue it, even though it had been previously cast.

"I made a backup just in case," I said, handing one to Theia and pocketing the other. "I know I must be cautious even when crafting from infinite resources. As they say, nothing in life ever truly comes free."

We were fitted in protective gear—either full hazmat suits or only simple filtration masks—to breathe properly despite the scratchy bits of dust. Graffiti covered nearly everything, and the room was filled with the strong smell of paint.

I pointed at what was left behind.

"They must have done some of this recently. Maybe they heard us up above when we were attacked. The sounds likely gave them a heads-up that others were coming. They're probably waiting for us."

CASTIN

Night-Morning-Afternoon

CHAPTER TEN: SEQUENCE

"I THINK THE MESSAGE THEY'RE TRYING TO send is loud and clear," Theia said, her sights fixed on something, and we gathered around to see what had caught her attention. Across from us, on a wall leading to level two, there was a crude depiction of a hangman spray-painted in red. The stick figure's head was depicted as dangling from a rope, with its body in several pieces on the ground. Bold letters beside it read:

GET OUT

"That's exactly what we're trying to do," I remarked. *I really hope that none of them recognize me. If only I still had my hat right now. I hope that Elijah hasn't lost it.* "The way we came in is blocked off, and there was a cave-in when we tried to get through it. There's no way to go back, even if we wanted to."

Everyone took turns examining the graffiti up close, likely checking for hidden symbols or analyzing the threatening message's context.

"Something bad is going to happen," Cam said, his voice tense.

"Why do you say that?" Abela asked, looking at him as if she was surprised at what he said.

"Just a feeling."

He wasn't wrong. The Drifters were not the type to be trifled with. I knew from experience. Let's just say I didn't always have the best reputation. Over the years, I'd encountered others who had trust issues with me and wouldn't take my word for anything. Those who had seen me brandish my guns might have thought I was unhinged. Breaking the rules was what allowed me to survive, doing things that others found too difficult.

I didn't earn my tattoos by following the rules.

I played the role that some needed me to in order to avoid getting caught. Appearing focused on my career kept the law from catching up to me. I figured that the rule-breakers wouldn't give me away because they didn't want to get caught either, you know?

Part of me wanted to ask Tule about that since she seemed to deal with similar issues, but I never did. I feared she might expose me. She once pretty much admitted to me that the agency threatened to go after her family in the past. *I've always been aware of their corruption, but that is too far.*

I had to say goodbye to mine when I signed on and my fingerprint patterns were collected, but I made it undoubtedly clear to my supervisors that the only thing they couldn't do was harm my loved ones. I'd have to take any fall or hit before them, even if they hardly knew who I was anymore. Working all hours since graduating created that distance. I still knew myself, despite those who only saw me by name.

Since an initial desire to work by myself, my cover about my involvement with magic had been blown. The only thing the Frontier didn't know was my previous associations with others who hadn't been caught. But there was one secret no one had uncovered yet, not even the other Magic Wielders, and I wasn't sure how they'd react when they found out.

I was hiding the fact that I was always a Drifter.

So, despite Cam's concerns over the threatening messages left by my secret second family, we proceeded to the second floor. It was more cluttered than the previous one. We were only two levels away from the exit. We spent a few minutes exploring. Our candles illuminated the room just enough to see what—or who—we were approaching. *They're going to strike at any moment. Gotta be ready for whatever happens.*

"How about we just go down to the first now?" Cam suggested, breaking the silence. "Why waste time looking around when we could head to the base—"

His lantern fell with a random and loud thud, directly followed by a series of chilling noises.

"Cam?" Trav called out, watching as it rolled across the floor. He used his own light to investigate what had happened.

He slowly lifted the lantern to reveal that Cam had vanished, seemingly disappearing into the darkness.

Trav's body went rigid as he raised his hands and took a few steps away from the library's far left side.

A warped circle, resembling one of the Frontier's portals, came into view. It not only made a vacuum-like noise but also pulled in anyone nearby with a strong suction. All the Forgotten members who had been with us were swept away in an instant, going into the void before I could say a word. They disappeared in front of Theia, the Librarian, and me.

Have no clue how they're going to handle this with me. So many screwed-up things had already happened, but this was bringing on one of the most intense waves of anxiety I'd ever experienced. Two of my worlds were about to collide, worlds that should have never known about one another in the first place. *Time for this all to go from bad to much worse!*

I knew that panicking would get me nowhere. I'd never given up on any mission before. Quitting wasn't an option where I came from. Every memory left permanent markers on my skin as various tattoos.

They didn't just represent certain skills; they were key markers of my magic level. Forty. I'd just reached it a few days before Zekiel arrived on the mud. Everyone involved with magic had their own level, even if they were novices or just unaware of it. Like me, many of them who knew kept it a secret, which prevented our weapons and gear from being stolen, as their substantial value was hidden from those desperate for luxury items.

Bay dollars became as scarce as morals over time.

The early days in the city were full of bandits and mercenaries. I could no longer join the groups I once used to run with when I decided to work for the Frontier. It was a choice I could never undo—a life signed away. *At least we lawbreakers believe in freedom.*

When Theia fell into a mud hole, I knew I had to help out. I tried to downplay how worried I was when she thanked me earlier, but deep down, the thought of her dying in those lonely tunnels was devastating. Some deserved to meet that end, but not her, especially not those who were like family or friends to me. We needed to look out for each other, something I had grown to understand in a short amount of time.

The only thing I truly believed in was magic, after all.

Coming face to face with my old gang of Drifters made me wonder how things were going up above for those on the foundation of Salt Crest. *They can't be lost. Especially Tule. I hope one day she'll understand that I wasn't ever against what she would talk about.*

I had to stop dwelling on what I couldn't change and instead on handling the immediate problems. It was not so much about escaping the tunnels—which would be the easy part—but rather talking to Bex, one of the head leaders of the Drifters, who was definitely about to recognize my stupefied look.

"Those portals are what the Frontier calls a punishment for not playing by their meaningless rules," Bex said, emerging from a hiding place under one of the tables. "You three are lucky you weren't on the wrong side of the room." Her dark green and brown armor was a mismatched collection of various materials, and she kept her identity concealed with a black full-face tactical gas mask, like the rest. The Drifters' outfits utilized shards and poles of broken metal, used as shields and weapons, kind of like Tule's.

"Why would they do that to them?" Theia asked, seeming as though she was fighting off memories of her own portal encounters, I was sure she had many.

Bex took extra time to walk around us. "It happens to those who have experience with Forced Evolutionary Magic. It's something that no one else can use, apparently, besides them. Not that they even know how to wield it properly. They keep messing up and then taking it out on others. That's why we Drifters continuously choose freedom. We broke the chains to make our own laws and land." As she reached the middle of the room and spotted me, her expression shifted. "Castin? What are you doing here? I can't believe this. You really are one of them now."

"Had to pay the bills... alright?" I shook my head and insisted, "I'm not, though. You have to trust me. I've been..." I glanced at Theia and the Librarian before dropping my shoulders. "Pretending. No one else knows I'm a Drifter. I had to do what I needed to in order to survive. Please understand. I've been conducting magic in secrecy amongst other things."

Bex removed part of her mask, revealing her tan, scar-covered skin. She was a tall and strong woman, and many were intimidated by her fighting experience and unwavering confidence. I was always inspired by her. "You know that you don't have to do that. Magic isn't something the Frontier owns, no matter how much they try. We took control of this place down here. They tried to take it back, but we won. How do you think we've managed to stay alive despite the ocean swallowing up the surrounding mud at night?"

"You actually cast a spell to protect Old Crow?"

"Yes. The agency has tried sending some of their shady crew down here periodically during the day to try to kill us off, but they fail or get lost every time." Bex pointed to some of the shelves that looked to have items belonging to one of the teams from up above.

Theia and the Librarian, standing just a few steps away, gasped as they listened to Bex and me catch up.

I'd suspected this of my coworkers due to things I'd read, but inquired more, "The scientists that they told us went missing were ones they forced to the tunnels?"

She nodded at the gear and scattered items that sat in between books. "Yeah. They made them come down here and forgot about their existence. The ones wearing purple who represent Euphrasia Arms... At least you aren't one of them. I can't stand their know-it-all attitude. Their swords are impressive, though, yet they have taken down a few of our own."

I tightened my fists. "Please don't tell me who. I can't deal with that knowledge right now."

"I won't," Bex assured me. "I want you to stay standing too. But Castin, you have to make a choice. I can't, in good conscience, let you out of these tunnels if you're going above to serve the wrong side—the one that seeks to destroy and steal from our own." Her brown hair she kept short was covered in layers of dust just as mine had become.

At that moment, around twelve other Drifters, fully armed and concealed from head to toe, emerged from various corners of the library. They came out from behind bookshelves of all types, surrounding Theia, the Librarian, and me. Each carried an array of weapons, reflecting the Drifters' lack of division. Chivs, guns, throwables—it didn't matter. As long as you remained loyal to the crew, you were considered family.

I had absolutely no idea what to say. Bex made it sound far simpler than it had really been. "You can't put me on the spot like this, alright?"

"Just let us go back to Salt Crest, please," Theia pleaded, stepping forward beside me. "We're running out of time! Something very bad is going to happen up there soon, and we need to get back to help the others."

"Yeah," the Librarian added. "Look, I see that this is complicated, with you running into Castin again. But we need to get up above to help innocent people who can't handle what the Frontier is putting them through on their own. You have to understand."

Bex turned to look at our friends. Some chuckled, while others were only staring me down. "What? You really think we're just going to let you all walk through the exit like that? It's not that simple."

"We don't want to fight," the Librarian stated.

"Well, that's how we do things around here, isn't it?" Bex replied with an authoritative grin, turning back to me. "Castin, I think it's time for you to face your fears. I remember them from your early mercenary days. Initiation was a struggle for you... wasn't it?"

I was sweating out of pure worry despite how cold it was. *Here comes everything getting a whole lot worse.* "You're going to make me do it again?"

"Of course. But this time, you will have help to survive until the end, yet I can't say how much."

Cheers erupted from my fellow Drifters as some clapped their hands, and gave high-fives. "Been waiting for this to take place again! Finally!"

"Castin, what are they talking about?" Theia asked from my left side, her hand resting on her sword's handle.

"I'll explain later," I replied in a hushed tone.

The Librarian stood tall. "I refuse to participate. I only use swords and my tools. I will not be facing any problems with the Frontier."

Bex guffawed. "The two of you are wearing black. It's clear you don't care what they think of you anyway. If you're true lawbreakers, then actually be some. Let's put your strength to the ultimate test. There are no unnecessary hoops to jump through down here. That's not how we Drifters handle things."

My original crew began laying out a variety of guns on the surrounding tables: pistols, shotguns, submachine guns, and countless more. They stood ready, waiting again for Bex to explain the test.

"Just play along, alright?" I said to Theia and the Librarian. "I won't hurt either of you, even if they try to force me to. Got it? Just... ugh... trust me on this."

"That gray is a disgrace. So led astray," I heard one of the others muttering to someone else behind my back.

"If you all can complete one round of our special tournament, then you can walk freely," Bex said with a smile at all of the illegal weaponry before us.

"How about you just let us go?" I asked. "What will carrying this out accomplish right now?"

"We have our own set of rules that you already know about, Castin," Bex replied with a hint of frustration in her voice. "I suggest you play along. You've sold out to the Frontier. I've been hiding my anger about this so far, but it needs to be released."

I knew there'd be some serious repercussions from my choices. I just didn't expect it to be like this, and so soon.

"You're really going to attack someone from your group?" Theia asked, disbelief evident in her tone.

"You of all people should understand what it's like to be forced into things you don't want to do," Bex implied that she knew of Theia's past with Elijah, something I discovered too much about. "Oh, that's right, *you* were the one forcing someone else's hand."

I was well-versed in both of their journals, which had some pretty intense moments. I wasn't sure how they had reintegrated into society after everything they'd been through. It seemed advantageous for them compared to those who had recently joined us and were less desensitized to curses and violence.

"Tell us the rules, please," the Librarian said urgently. "Let's do what we need to so we can get back to Salt Crest in time."

"This is going to be Castin's choice," Bex said. "Either you face the challenge now or later."

I'll need to find a way around this to not be punished for the choices I have made. "Later," I said firmly.

"Go on your way, then," Bex said. "Just remember, there's a group guarding the exit. They don't let anyone through without a fight, no matter who they are."

"Well, if they know that I'm a Dri—"

"They don't care."

I wasn't looking forward to the next encounter with Bex. A lot of fighting was to come, I was going to be put through the ringer for some of the hasty decisions I had made when I was tight on money and disregarding several morals. We finally left to reach the last level and get out of the tunnels. I felt trapped in my thoughts and barely spoke to Theia or the Librarian. Despite tuning them out, I appreciated their gratitude for my choice to spare them from the challenge.

"Theia? Where did you go?" he suddenly called out, receiving no response, then turned to look at me. "I thought she was trailing nearby? You appear to have your attention focused on other matters, but I'd appreciate it if you help me see what happened? She seemingly disappeared within the last few minutes."

I did what I could to help him look around, concerned as she seemed to be having issues with her nerves. "Yeah, sure thing, I'll check the bathrooms."

"Theia?!" the Librarian called out again.

Within a few stressful seconds, she stepped into the center of the first floor we had just gone down to. "Hey, I'm right here. Sorry about that."

"How did you get here before us?" the Librarian asked, puzzled.

Theia looked concerned as our attention fell on her. She stood next to the secretary's table, nervously fiddling with unused pens as she thought of what to say.

"If telling us what happened will put us in more danger, how about you *not* say anything?" I suggested. "I saw you, Theia." I gave her a nod. *Get it?*

"Let's just keep moving on," she replied tersely.

The main level had been turned into a Drifter camp. They had made rooms out of the shelves, chairs, tables, and repurposed the books. None of them, including me, had any interest in poring over crusty and stained literary texts.

The Librarian spoke next, "I think I know the fastest way to the basement from here."

There were no more traps near our feet, but instead, the bulk of what once made the library's contents was trashed and scattered around. The space was never given the opportunity to be used for its purpose, as the Drifters had explored and claimed it.

My rebel group had used some of the stolen resources from the Forgotten that they murdered. The three of us came across what had been left behind and stopped a few times to collect what we could fit into our limited inventory.

We continued on foot to what we hoped would be our final destination before finally reaching freedom. I yearned to breathe outside air again, even if it smelled of salty ruins, and to feel the sun's rays through the clouds.

Freedom was close, but another pack of Drifters also wasn't far as they lurked in rooms and shadows. To protect themselves, they didn't place any traps on the first floor. The head mercenary outliers didn't seem to think that anyone would make it far enough to reach their home base.

Once noise came from the attic, they had moved quickly to assemble a survival puzzle for our group to get through to reach the basement. Many Drifters were likely angry after discovering Theia was alive under rubble and probably knew she had overheard much of what they had said and done. They were waiting for us to get closer to their hiding place.

I was the first to notice string tied around the base of the floorboards and legs of furniture. I crouched and held my lantern closer. "Hold on... Huh, it's just some fishing line that's not connected to anything. It must only be here to distract us from something else."

We all stepped over it and followed the Librarian underneath a sign hanging in the hallway that stated:

EXIT

I smiled. "Maybe this wasn't so bad after all."

Then, I felt a gun press against my left arm. A Drifter had emerged from what I thought was a vacant room and kept her finger planted on the trigger. "Wait," she commanded.

I raised my gun in response in a split second.

A handful of other Drifters peeked out from behind the nearby doors and stood at either end of the narrow hallway.

"The Frontier doesn't let just *anyone* approach their front gates," the Drifter said. "They have a code requirement to pass through this exit. Only those who know it are allowed to leave."

I pointed to my snowy mountain tattoo. "Well, that shouldn't be a problem. I work for them."

"Anyone could've gotten that ink job."

"Maybe if they can pass the sequence test?" a taller Drifter with a cage for a mask suggested. "The gate key to Euphrasia. Only twelve people know it."

I recited, "Three. Four. Five."

A stranger lowered her rifle. "How do you know that?"

"Was from a journal," I replied.

"What's the three-digit encryption code?"

"Four. Two. Nine." They fell silent, so I took that as a cue to continue and reached for the doorknob that led to the basement. "Sounds like we can move on?"

Suddenly, a Drifter lunged at me with a sharp blade, aiming for my gut.

"I told you the codes!" I shouted as I blocked his attack and disarmed him with a swift kick to his knee. He crumpled to the ground. "You sure you want to go after me like that?"

Theia was making her way over to help defend me when another Drifter tripped her from the sidelines, causing her to stumble. Her sword clattered loudly against the concrete as it fell from her hands.

The Librarian rushed to help her up after she had fallen onto the dirty floor and scraped her palms. "What's wrong with all of you?" he demanded.

"We hadn't confirmed the second code yet!" a stranger snapped. "You can't go through unless the sequence is verified!"

The surrounding strangers kept the exit blocked.

"You have to get through us to go outside," one of them snarled in the hardly lit room.

"What about the code?" I asked.

"It's correct," the other rebel confirmed. "But I don't trust you. We're not letting you through."

"Where else are we supposed to go then?" I asked, frustrated at them unnecessarily complicating things.

"How about six feet under where you're standing? It'll be easy to prepare your graves," the Drifter said coldly.

The man beside her added, "We won't make them graves. Let's be honest and get this done before other *citygoers* show up."

Suddenly, everyone's weapons were drawn. The Librarian was the first to strike, killing two from the group with his sword as he overpowered their relatively slow attack speeds. *They must be new.*

I pummeled several of them with bullets, taking down those not wearing extra gear first with headshots until I was nearing needing to reload my supply again.

The Librarian pulled out his book, ink, and feather, and started writing a command. "I've only heard epic tales of this, but I've never tried it before." He showed us the phrase:

F.E.M.: ShieldCover (MaxDuration)

A semi-translucent light blue bubble formed around him, and the rest of us stepped inside. Theia was the second to join, followed by me. The Drifters' bullets ricocheted off the mystic barrier, but we Magic Wielders were still able to push through and attack. The Librarian noticed Theia struggling to use her weapon and me getting aggravated as I ran out of bullets. He pulled out his book again and showed me what he'd written on the next page:

F.E.M.: AmmoRefill

Just as the book's cover had delivered masks to us, boxes of ammo, throwables, and modification attachments appeared through it.

I was beside myself with relief. "Thank you so much!"

It wasn't long before I had replenished what I needed to take out the rest of the Drifters. They yelled angrily as they were shot and stabbed with precision and force. Taking out some of my own to survive was something I had unfortunately done before, but never this many, not like this. Blood splattered in the air, and cries for help echoed. A few remaining at the back of the hallway tried to flee or surrender. I didn't let them. *They'll kill us once we have our backs turned to get out of here. I just know it.* I ran out of the shield, following them as a few dropped their weapons.

"Just go out the exit!" one begged. "Please, please don't hurt me! I didn't choose to be here!"

"Don't care." There was no emotion in my voice as I shot him. "Goes for all of you."

Soon, they were all dead, and Theia's voice cracked as she spoke, "We have to go through the exit."

I was the last to leave the bloody mess of a hallway, stained and tarnished with ruthless memories of needless violence. We stepped over each corpse, creating distance from one another as they lay in pools of their own blood. Even for me, it was a rough sight.

I did my best not to look down at them, silently paying what felt like such twisted respects in my head. *How can I mourn losses that I had to cause?* I wasn't sure how I was going to live with myself, but I had to figure that out later due to the time-sensitive issues at hand.

Theia and the Librarian were in the front, and he noticed her rubbing her hands on the exposed parts of her arms. "Are you doing okay?"

"Y-yeah, it's just my nerves," she replied shakily.

They slowed their steps for a moment, allowing me to pass while he spoke with her, presumably returning the armor after he took it off. Once they exchanged a few secret words, they fell back in line behind me just as I reached the exit of the tunnels.

The metal door creaked as I opened it, revealing the muddy climb to higher ground. Sunlight crept down the path and cast rays of warmth on my skin. I could smell fresh air and took in deep breaths of it.

While we climbed, I reviewed the resources we had left from the tunnels. We all took inventory, ensuring we knew exactly how many food packages, water bottles, and medkits we had left from the Forgotten. There wasn't much left, only enough to last a few more days with barely any resources beyond that.

Despite being achy and sore, we made it to the top. Each step was more painful than the last. The air felt warm on my sensitive face. We helped each other climb the final stretch of mud to the dirt. Finally, we emerged from the pressurized passageways and faced the largest issue at hand.

Saving Salt Crest City.

We could see the city rising in the distance.

Below it, we spotted three other figures.

We started shouting, waving our hands, and running on the mud while avoiding holes.

But as we got closer, it became clear.

They couldn't see us.

ZEKIEL

Evening-Night

CHAPTER ELEVEN: LAST SIGHT

IT WAS DOWN ON THE MUD THAT TULE
joined Elijah and me on the outskirts to defend the
perimeter from an oncoming sell attack. We walked
side by side, my sword's curved blades leaving lines
behind in the mud when my posture faltered. The
clouds formed a giant circle around the moon, casting
an ominous shadow. Terror was on the rise for those
back inside the gates, who were equipping armor,
sharpening melee weapons, and loading their guns. A

giant rope, tied to one of the beams, provided a way for us to climb up or down as the city rose higher.

Theia's whereabouts were still unknown, along with Castin and the Librarian, who had gone to the tunnels to save her. Elijah went in the opposite direction, insisting he could handle fighting off the oncoming hordes on his own and seeming distraught.

"Thank you for saving us with the flowers." I walked close to Tule. "I can't believe I ever took the life I used to have for granted. Life with Jas— My past. So many things I should've done, said, and *not* done."

"You're welcome. Thank you for supporting my efforts." She couldn't stop looking at me for a few moments with care in her eyes. "I've been meaning to ask... what was it you did before you got involved with magic?"

"I worked a lot of twelve-hour days in construction. I've always wanted to be an architect, but I stopped pursuing that years ago when a loved one of mine passed away. A woman who I hoped to have a future with. I never thought that I would ever lose her." I glanced down at Tule to see her reaction.

"I'm sorry to hear that." She looked away with a sorrowful expression.

I have to see whatever positives I can despite the past. I can be free. "Jasmine always supported my dreams, even when I didn't support myself. At least I know she'd be proud to see where I am now. She and some of my best friends passed away. May they rest in peace."

There were a few minutes of silence between us. As I walked, I recalled a letter that I had memorized:

Zekiel,

I know you want space from me, and I understand why, but please know that I am worried about you. Your distance has been hard on me. I can't imagine what you're going through, but you don't have to go through it alone. I am always here for you no matter what. After all these years, I still care about you the same way. Nothing that happens will ever change how I feel about you. You're loved. Please don't push me away again.

Storms will eventually subside.

-Saige

How much do we still not know that's out there? From this evolutionary magic? What other curses have to be broken? What else are we going to have to do?

"I should've mentioned this earlier," Tule said, breaking the silence with a tense tone. "There's something I need to tell you about certain parts of the work I do. I didn't share the entire truth about how everyone got here. I'll keep my confession short..."

"'Confession'? What is it that you did?" I asked, speaking with curiosity as we continued onwards.

"I, well, sort of used magic to get some others to agree to join us here. We were desperate for help. Experiments went wrong. So many lawsuits. I don't have enough time to explain everything." She put a hand near her mouth, waiting for my reaction.

What is she telling me right now? "Are you serious? I don't know what to say. What did you use?"

Tule pointed towards the city. "It's a mixture mentioned in a book I read. There was no other choice. I, and everyone else who appeared here, became stuck. We tried to only get Theia to help, but that didn't work. Elijah couldn't assist either. There's no way almost anyone in their right mind would have agreed to this."

"So, when were you going to tell me this?" The shocking sound of Castin's words cut through the air.

How long has he been following behind us?

Tule was visibly shaking at the sudden confrontation. "I know how this sounds, believe me, but I did nothing wrong! Let me explain what happened when I arrived b-before we met here! This is a misunderstanding! I'm sorry for how it sounds!"

"You think I'm going to put this to rest with a 'sorry'? That's the kind of person you are, Tule? Was I drugged? What did you do?" His voice got deeper.

She raised hers over the roar of warm rain pouring in unison with the sells' erratic footsteps, "I'm not! It isn't what it seems! I'll have to explain later!"

"You don't know the whole story and neither do I!" I said, trying to diffuse the situation as I noticed the others emerging from the direction of the tunnels. *They're alive!* "We need to focus on fighting whatever else is coming! There are still more of them heading this way! We'll die if we're distracted!"

He took a step closer towards both of us with a shrug. "You want me to put this on the back burner?"

Tule's voice shook as she answered, "Just hear me out later, okay? I have only done what I thought was the best for everyone! We're allies and are members of the same Front—"

Castin drew his double-barreled shotgun.

I stepped in between them and drew my sword. "Put the gun down! Don't resort to using that!"

"Why?" Castin sprang forward, seizing the sword that Tule held unsteadily. "To make this fair since you're too scared to fight with one? For that matter, who's to say that you aren't wearing the key right now?"

"Are you talking about my armor?" We faced off for a few tense seconds. "You think that I have it?"

"Yeah." He gave me a stare worth a thousand words with a threatening tone, "Prove that the symbol isn't in it!"

Tule jumped in. "No, Zekiel, he's tricking yo—"

But before she could finish, I took off the part that guarded my heart.

Castin lunged quickly, driving the rigid blade into the exposed part of my chest. Blood poured down my abdomen as my skin was painfully torn open. It began bubbling green. The horn blared brokenly as the moon rose. A loud cry filled the sky through the vintage speaker, and stars glowed like white paint flicked across a dark gray canvas. A roar echoed as my blood hit the ground.

The sea dragon awoke, sensing the emblem nearby.

We began running for our lives back to the city. As we ran, I saw the Librarian and Theia climbing the rope to escape the mud. Elijah, far from them, chose to hack away at the oncoming sells rather than join them on safer ground. Avoiding what looked like sunken holes in the mud, I kept a steady pace towards the gates, trying to outrun the mutants. I helped Tule to the rope first, then went up myself, followed by Castin.

Screams of terror erupted as the leviathan emerged to attack, its neck towering over everyone, with nearly boiling water cascading off its scales. I pressed my hands to my ears, desperately trying to block out the deafening roar. Almost all of the sells had gone underwater as mud crumbled beneath their sharp talons. People ran for cover, either inside buildings or into the nearest alleyways. Shots were fired, but they barely made a dent. The dragon followed the trail of poisoned blood seeping from my gaping chest wound.

Tule immediately took cover as the leviathan crashed through entire buildings, its massive wings causing partial flooding with the water it displaced. The wind whipped around us as it flew menacingly.

Castin and I ran frantically to the other side of the city, dodging fallen crates, other survivors, and decorative structures that had toppled over in our way. We got to the edge at the same time and had no choice but to climb up and over the tenth section. The impact of falling into the ocean from the height the city had risen could shatter every bone in a person's body, but there was no time to find another route.

"We have to jump back down!" Castin shouted, pointing to a bulk of mud. "We'll swim over there!"

Without hesitation, we leaped off the edge, away from the sea dragon. I hit the wet surface with a loud splash. The force knocked the air out of my lungs as I fell into the warm, eel-infested territory and coughed up salty water. My skin stung as I swam towards the mud. The dragon charged after us, swimming beneath the water before rising towards higher grounds.

Theia jumped down from the back part of the gate as a shortcut to get over to us. She fell into the ocean within seconds, stunned, and gasped out over and over again for air. Once she reached the mud and was able to stand, she threw her armor in front of Castin and me. "Put it on! It'll make you invisible!"

We had only moments to decide who would wear it.

"Do it!" Castin demanded.

Heaps of mud and water hurtled towards us. I grabbed the armor, undid its fastenings, and put it on. I closed my eyes, trying to block out the dragon's cries and screams of those witnessing the chaos. Jasmine was the only person on my mind as I felt power surge through me. I held my sword so tightly that my blood flow was restricted. Placing my other hand on Castin's shoulder to help him, we suddenly went invisible.

Theia could apparently no longer see either of us. *I thought only one person could be invisible at a time? Whose power was I given?* I quickly realized... *Saige's.*

The city continued to rise too high, making it impossible for anyone else to jump down. The leviathan, snarling in defeat, sank into the waters, waiting to attack again.

I made us visible once more, our situation growing more dire. Salt Crest was moments away from being consumed by poison.

Castin ran towards the rope, which was being lifted higher into the sky with each passing moment. The city floated out of reach like a balloon caught in the wind. The frayed edges of the rope barely grazed his fingertips as he struggled to grab hold. "No! Wait!" he shouted, but despite his attempts, it was too far away.

The mist grew into a heavy fog of forest green that swallowed the gray that once warmly encompassed everyone. I felt myself shrinking below Tule, the distance between us growing with each passing second. She waved her arms frantically as she was ripped up into the lethal atmosphere. Tears filled my eyes as we were pulled farther apart.

I can't lose another friend, they're so hard to find.

Rain poured as I dropped my cumbersome sword, and blood returned to my hands. As I released my grip... I saw smoke curling from my palms again—something I hadn't seen since first arriving at Salt Crest City in the armory. *No... what is happening?* The smoke was purple this time, and flames began to flicker. *No! Wait! I have my abilities back?* The rain extinguished the fire, but I could feel it still within me. *Why do I have supernatural abilities? For what purpose?*

Hot droplets of rain traveled down my hair and stung my wounded chest. I felt lightheaded as blood poured out of me. My leather armor bore the marks of near-death experiences, just as scars covered my skin. I had survived by not giving up and embracing the magic that I, and everyone else, depended on to live. I took off my drenched top and held the armor as the horn blared the final countdown.

THREE MINUTES REMAINING

At least I've been able to keep Tule safe so far. I took in what I feared would be my last sight of her. She looked at me, her trembling fingers digging into her wet curls. The air turned greener, and I could no longer see or hear anyone else from above, their chilling screams fading as they were ripped from safety.

Despite not wanting to fight for my life in the past, at that moment, all I could feel was a profound fear of losing it.

Castin and Elijah were nearby, also struggling to remain upright on the rumbling mud. I overheard some of their shouting. Apparently, Elijah had accidentally lost his hat and was trying to apologize for the mistake. Castin wanted to hear nothing of it, though, and tried to dismiss him since it didn't matter under our current circumstances. *I'd be trying to get my mind off what's happening right now too if I could. This might be the end for us.*

I felt as though I would soon be swallowed alive. At any moment, the dragon could burst from beneath us with a hungry vigor to kill again. Strong winds whipped past us, causing me to slide as I moved toward them. I hissed out in pain from the burning in my chest as toxic raindrops continued to damage the deep cut.

Maybe I should give this to him or Castin... "Want to try its power? Mine won't do anything now!" I yelled, tossing the armor onto the ground, where it landed with a wet thud.

It's changing! Moonlight poured over Elijah, Castin, Theia, and me as we exchanged worried looks. The mud was completely turning into the ocean beneath our feet. Our only option was for someone to cast a spell. *There's no way we can survive this without harnessing something else!* "One of you needs to try it!"

"Not me!" Castin yelled back. "Elijah should!"

There was a collective understanding that we couldn't waste time by going back and forth arguing or asking questions. Elijah nodded and ran toward where it was despite the risk of pockets of air or water underneath the mud like a minefield. Some of the foundation started to crumble away beneath his feet as he quickly equipped the armor.

For a whole minute, no spells were cast. As Salt Crest City was rising in my peripheral vision, I counted the remaining time in my mind. *Tule! The Librarian!* Flashes of everyone else appeared before me as my lip quivered at the grim realization of what was happening in the neon-green sky. Imminent death. Losing those I cared about once more.

"Nothing is happening! I—I only have thirty seconds!" Elijah shouted hoarsely at the sky, his voice cracking with desperation. "I can't do it! Nothing is working!"

"Try to stay calm! We still have some time!" Castin replied. I'd never seen him look so powerless before. "Okay?"

I wanted to speak, but I had no idea what to say.

"Nothing is happeni—" Elijah's shouting faltered as he looked down. His index finger began to glow.

TULE

Night

CHAPTER TWELVE: SWITCHING SIDES
THERE WAS HARDLY ANY TIME LEFT TO LIVE.

Everything was a blur through my burning tears. We were about to be killed by the suffocating poison, while those below would be stranded on a minefield of treacherous mud. Time was almost up. Then, out of seemingly nowhere, a brilliant light engulfed us as a teleportation spell was miraculously cast before the countdown ended. *Who did that? Will we all be okay?*

Instead of succumbing to an unfortunate demise, some of us were teleported miles away to the Hot Springs. I had only ever read warnings about them and how they were closed off to the public due to the restrictive layout of the area. Upon arriving, I realized that what I thought I knew about them wasn't completely accurate. What *was* the same, though, was that they were still unsafe to visit and bubbling over. Despite the risks, I was thankful to be there. We at least had a chance to travel somewhere safer with no timer looming over us. I finally let out a deep breath.

Elijah had a hard time explaining why we hadn't ended up in safer parts of Earth like the others, but I didn't need an explanation. The magic within *us* ran deep. And apparently, the Springs was where we were called to next. After a bit of disorientation, I realized that I was there with Zekiel, Castin, Elijah, Theia, and someone else I hadn't met yet who stood mysteriously.

We all were only a few feet away from each other on light brown ground that had little cracks in it. No one said anything at all for a few moments. I was in so much shock that I was left entirely speechless. *Is anyone hurt? I wonder what happened down below?*

Zekiel stepped away from us for a few minutes, saying he wanted some privacy, and tried to hide the cut on his chest. I could tell he was in a lot of pain.

"I'm sorry about that, by the way," Castin said loudly enough for us all to hear. When he received no response, he turned to me and added, "Can you let him know later that I *really* am sorry? It was all a misunderstanding. I know that you didn't choose to put me through any of this. Your hand was forced. I know, and believe, that now. Zekiel wouldn't have saved my life if the former had been true. I can't undo what happened back there, but I can at least give some advice. You should talk to the Librarian and see if he could help with the wound. It actually turns out that he has the gift of healing when wearing the armor."

I spotted the man he was gesturing to, noting how handsome he looked as he leaned beside one of the trees, absorbed in writing in a book. It seemed like he was using the moonlight to illuminate his work in the dark forest with ink and a quill to passionately create.

I walked over. "Hi. I'm sorry to interrupt you."

"No need to apologize," he said smoothly, putting his things away and extending his hand, which I gladly shook. "You can call me the Librarian. I've seen you around Crow Library. It's really nice to meet you."

"My name is Tule. Nice to meet you, too."

He pushed his glasses to the top of his head, sweeping his long black hair out of his face. I found myself momentarily lost in his deeply contemplative gaze as he waited patiently for me to speak again.

"Someone in our group is hurt—Zekiel. He was stabbed just before we were teleported from the city. The blade was my sword, one I killed some sells with, it got stolen. Now the wound seems to be infected."

The Librarian took a few seconds to process all I shared before replying, the look on his face equally showed concern and care as he gave a reassuring nod. "I'm very sorry to hear about that. I can definitely help. I'll go ask Elijah if I could borrow the armor."

"Thank you so much." I already hoped to talk more with him in the future. His very full bookbag and calming presence were extremely intriguing to me.

"You're welcome," he said with a smile before heading over to the others. "I'm around if you need any help, something to read, or someone to talk to."

Theia, Elijah, and Castin discussed the final moments of Salt Crest City while the Librarian changed into the magical armor behind some trees and joined Zekiel, who was still alone. I watched the healing process from a distance, mesmerized by the yellow light emanating from the man's steady hands.

How is he doing that? I've only ever read about healers who can harness elemental properties through their bodies. It was nearly impossible to take my eyes off of him. *He seems so amazing. What else can he do? I wonder what manuscripts he has? Some seem familiar.*

The excitement and happiness of escaping the countdown to disaster was blissful... until it wasn't. After around ten minutes with a few of us going back and forth about what we were going to do next, a bittersweet feeling of survival mixed with impending doom hung in the air as time passed.

Several loud whooshes eventually sounded off in the snowy distance, growing closer with each moment as we traveled on foot. The wind blew stronger with each gust, and it felt as though something was forcefully disrupting the atmosphere around us. Suddenly, a flock of crows erupted from the nearby trees and flew away, except for one that appeared to have mutated and flew past us at increasing speeds.

"Did either of you notice that the crow was missing in the library earlier?" the Librarian asked Theia and Castin, brushing mud off his coat and keenly keeping his eyes on the sky. "I thought that it would have been directly across from the front desk, but it wasn't there."

Castin shrugged. "I figured it must've been buried somewhere. Why? What do you think this means?"

"Almost everything was replicated exactly from the library in the city. This must be it... It came to life! I've never encountered this type of occurrence, I thought that the use of these certain spells was now forbidden!" The Librarian pointed towards it as it headed our way.

Massive wings carried the bird through the air as it flew around us from the direction of the Hot Springs. *Maybe it's not going to be hostile?* Its cawing shook the ground and trees for miles around. The mutant's beak was sharp, and its black eyes resembled shattered glass.

"Extra thankful for the ammo now!" Castin said. "Does anyone else want to use a gun? I can share."

Almost all of them responded with firm no's.

He sighed. "Come on. You'd rather risk dying?"

"You know that there's hardly any difference where we're from," I said. "For those who've already chosen their alliance, at least. We can't just switch sides back and forth."

"How will they even know? You act like they got cameras on us twenty-four-seven. The Frontier will have no idea, alright? Now how about you help me? You know… all that talk about working together?"

I looked at his immediate collection of well-maintained and pricy firearms: a rifle, a holstered pistol, and a shotgun among others. "I'll take the rifle."

Castin handed it to me alongside ammo without asking questions. I could tell that he was really distraught because he said nothing at all. His eyes were only focused on where he needed to aim. Everyone held their breaths, waiting and watching in silence.

Holding the gun and ammunition felt unsettling, but even more so with the unknown bird approaching.

I had to act fast despite the promised repercussions of my last-second actions. I fumbled with a couple of bullets while loading my gun, but I refrained from scolding myself; I was under so much pressure. We soon started firing at the massive crow from a distance, the sound of our shots echoing through the humid air.

Despite our efforts, we only managed to inflict minimal damage on its overgrown parasitic-ridden wings. The Librarian enchantingly wrote in his book, creating a safe place to retreat, and I stepped into the protective dome as soon as it was done forming.

"Everyone should stay inside!" he shouted, standing at the shield's center with outstretched arms.

The creature, wounded by our shots, screeched louder as some of its long black feathers fell to the ground. However, we were unable to greatly harm the crow. It flew away, scared off, just as the shield faded out of sight for its cooldown period. *We're all okay.*

After the unnerving ordeal, we made our way to our next destination, which ended up becoming another dangerously deadly journey—venturing through the Hot Springs. *This must be another location the higher-ups used to conduct experiments. Who knows what sorts of evidence they've tossed into these toxic waters? I'm sure they have their reasons for making sure no one comes here.*

"Those must be the Springs up ahead. Never thought I'd actually see them." Castin was the first to speak, his voice full of worry as the hot mist came into view.

"This can't be right," the Librarian muttered, flipping through one of his books. "These Springs are different from the ones described in the text. We won't be able to cross on foot. I'll have to make something."

I was impressed that he knew that. *Wow, he's well-read,* I thought as he pulled out a couple more titles to cross-reference his findings. *Why? To get where?* My thoughts were soon answered with just a few more steps, revealing a vast expanse beyond the horizon. Instead of several small springs, they had merged into a massive one.

"Do you all also see that building in the distance? Or do I need to get more water?" Theia asked, her lips chapped and her voice low from exhaustion.

I wordlessly handed her my last bottle to drink.

"Thank you," she mumbled gratefully.

"I see it too." The Librarian flipped to the next blank page within his book and took out the ink and feather from his coat pockets. "We have to cross over to the other side."

The silhouette of the building loomed eerily through the fog. It was multiple stories high and painted in a dirty off-white accompanied by an ominous shadow. The windows were all black and lined up perfectly in a row. A large gate wrapped around the perimeter, reminiscent of Salt Crest City, yet I sensed that the dangers there lurked from within rather than below.

"*That's* where we're going?" Zekiel asked, eyeing the building with concern.

Castin nodded to the Librarian. "What are you gonna write?"

He didn't answer at first, and we listened to the sound of his ink being scratched purposefully into the paper. There were still many pages of the book left for him to fill in. Then, he held up the page for us to see.

F.E.M.: Res/FwdBoatBox (6)

"No going back to that shield, eh?" Castin remarked. "Hope there's no ambush waiting for us."

The magical boat he had requested didn't arrive through the manuscript itself; instead, it was delivered in pieces from falling supply drops, parachuting down from a F.E.M. helicopter that was alerted. Each component landed softly, a series of gentle thuds marking their arrival. The box meant for the Springs was designed to stay put, but the Librarian cleverly modified his request to ensure that it was suited for the corrosive journey. It turned out to have been granted a resistance perk, making it indestructible to the chemicals left behind by ecological disaster.

The boat box was designed to only move forward. All of us climbed into it once it was assembled, mostly by the Librarian and Zekiel. The space was cramped, and Theia struggled the most to stay inside since she was the last to get in.

"Stay still please, okay? We'll make it over," I said, placing a hand on her arm as she was partially sitting on me and partly hanging onto the edge of the boat.

The customized hot tub pulled us along, and we were soon interrupted by schools of fish. A few sharp fins peeked out from the waters and circled us as we moved. Sweat dripped feverishly from my skin.

"No way!" Castin exclaimed as he saw his hat floating down the lake. He managed to grab it before it drifted too far. Surprisingly, the water didn't sting him.

Elijah let out a massive sigh of relief. "Wow."

Must be tied to him in some magical way.

Suddenly, something large bumped into the boat, tipping us to one side. We yelled, gripping the rusted metal we were practically encased in. The jolt sent Theia halfway off the edge. I quickly grabbed her torso, trying to hold onto her as carefully as I could.

"Hold on! It'll be okay!" I shouted.

My hands were sweaty, worsened by the metal armor I was wearing against the protective barrier of clothing. My grip was slipping, and Theia anxiously lost her hold on the box as it tilted side to side as if we were struck by a hard wave.

"I'm going to fall! Please, help!" she cried out.

Zekiel was closest to me and tried to assist, but leaning over to get a hold of her made the sway of the boat worse. He moved backwards, giving me space to manage the situation. With each passing second, sweat dripped from me, and I struggled to keep a grip on Theia, whose armor was slick with condensation from the mist. The metal felt hot and slippery under my fingers, making it even harder to hold on.

With a burst of strength, she managed to pull herself back into the boat. I gasped for air, realizing I had been holding my breath. "I'm glad you're okay," I said, relieved, before Theia thanked me profusely. I was shaking and decided to keep quiet until we reached the shore. Most of the others remained silent too, and a heavy wave of worry and shock slammed into my gut as the sky grew darker.

The land we were approaching was dotted with tall trees encircling a single building in the distance. Flickering lights shone through some of the windows, casting a glow that resembled television screens playing old black-and-white films.

"We're almost at the shore," Theia said weakly. "Let's meditate to pass the time and lower our stress."

"I can't promise I won't fall asleep," Castin grumbled from underneath his hat.

Everyone closed their eyes as Theia led us through a simple, yet effective, guided meditation. It was then that I experienced a small moment of peace as we were taken away from our reality for a while. Her voice was tired, but full of strength as she comforted and helped us until it trailed off when reaching a relaxed state. It was only when we opened our eyes that we realized she was no longer in the boat box. The alarming surprise settled in as we all exchanged glances, quickly grasping that she had somehow gone missing again.

"Theia!?" Elijah sprang into action, his hands hovering near the area where she had just been, as if hoping to uncover some trace of her presence.

"Guess it's time you all figure this out too," Castin said, pointing to the building. "Teleportation command. Same thing that happened earlier in Old Crow. Maybe ask the Librarian about how he did it."

Elijah glanced over at him with a puzzled face.

"When I helped her?" the Librarian asked as we finally reached the shore, holding his sword and bag.

"You must've granted her that perk back," Zekiel said, putting his face in his hands. "I've heard of healers who can provide boosts to others."

"This means Theia may be able to truly, finally, send us home. We may not need to enter that building, after all." Elijah was talking out loud to himself in a panic. "But the command seems to be working differently than usual. Wonder if it has to do with the aftermath of her injuries?"

We exited the boat to find ourselves facing a dense forest, with a building looming not far from it that we aimed to avoid. *I hope she's close by.* I could've sworn I heard a voice calling out from the trees as we approached them.

As if anticipating our needs, the Librarian pulled out his book once more and wrote a new command. He trailed behind us, rummaging in one of his pockets that rattled more than the others. It must have been where he stored bay dollars.

F.E.M.: NailGun (Mod: Screws/BayDollars)

With the words written and shared, he crafted something specifically for his own use. It was heavy, a big hunk of mismatching metal, a hybrid between a functioning tool — but also a deadly weapon. He filled its ammo compartment with a handful of screws that he probably had no other use for.

"What are you doing back there?" Zekiel asked.

The others, holding their swords or guns, were curious about the clinking sounds coming from his creation.

"Getting ready to fight. Just in case," he said, his hands balanced and thoughtfully placed as he worked.

The air was growing colder as we all spoke, and I felt like our words were unknowingly being listened to by something—or someone—in the darkness. A chill ran down my spine, and the hairs on the back of my neck stood up. *We need to be careful, the Frontier has probably already sent some staff after us. I'm sure they know that we've survived.* I grew nauseous with fear as the night drew to a close.

Everyone agreed to stay within a certain distance from one another while splitting up to search for Theia. With no light and limited resources, we had to move quickly. Drifters had painted graffiti symbols on the bark of each tree at its base, marking a trail to guide them back to where they came from. The artwork was in the form of various shapes and clouds outlined underneath them. Out of the corner of my eye, I could've sworn I saw someone silently gesture to another. *What if they were notified right away about our arrival once our boat reached the shore?*

My suspicions were proved to be true when rebels ambushed us. They had been waiting patiently for our group to venture deeper into the forest to attack. They got closer while we spoke of incriminating subject matters. There was apparently little they didn't hear.

A bright moon was on the rise in the starry sky as a grouping of Drifters charged towards me and the rest who'd dispersed amongst the trees. I heard their soft footsteps as they quietly maneuvered around thicker roots and fallen branches. Chills ran through my skin.

I started firing my gun, with Castin by my side, and saw Zekiel as he began slashing with his sword. My gun was tightly fitted with what I assumed was an extremely expensive suppressor. I could tell that the weapon was handled with great detail and oddly rare. My muffled shots inflicted serious damage on a few of them just as they started firing back. I ran out of ammo sooner than I expected. Castin was also running low, and when the Librarian noticed, he jumped in to help with his nail gun, which I was very grateful for.

Elijah was in the middle of the fray, his arm raised, as he sprinted past us. He attacked the Drifters with great force and what appeared to be practiced precision. One of them fell to the ground, knees first, as he pulled his blade out of their chest after a few rough tugs. As they bled out before him, he seemed disoriented. *Has he never killed someone else until now?*

Zekiel noticed Elijah standing frozen in place and helped take down the other rebels who had almost overtaken him in his distracted state. Soon, there was only one of our enemies left to fight. All of us—besides Elijah—cornered him with our weapons drawn as he began pleading for us to spare him.

"No! Wait! Don't hurt me, please!" the Drifter yelled through a dirty mask, his horror-stricken eyes visible through goggles that were glued to green fabric.

"We have no reason to trust you," Zekiel replied.

"But you need me alive! I know where Theia is! That woman you're looking for! I overheard some of what was said earlier." His hasty response was hoarse.

Elijah clenched his bloody fists. "Do you really know where she is?"

"Yeah?" The stranger replied with uncertainty, "W-we passed by her on our order to ambush you!?"

Castin snickered. "You're lying, aren't you? Why would you see her and not kill her? I'm sure that the you-know-who's have a kill-on-sight rule. Show us where she is while you still have a chance to."

We formed a well-armed circle around the Drifter, who raised his hands in surrender. "She disappeared into thin air before we could attack! I'll show you, but you have to promise not to kill me!" he begged more.

The others shrugged or nodded, but I remained still and in shock at everything that was unfolding.

"We'll see," Castin said, his gun trained on the Drifter's head as he led us through the forest. We walked through patches of darkness where trees with wide, thick branches blocked our view of the sky. Small fragments of moonlight revealed more symbols on the tree bases, and we started paying closer attention to the bark near our feet.

"Are you doing alright?" Zekiel whispered to me.

"Just a little nervous, that's all." *That's an understatement.* My fingers wavered, and I avoided eye contact. "I wonder what's going to happen next?"

He looked down at my snowy hand that was holding Castin's assault rifle with a hesitant grip. "It will be okay. We're about to meet up with Theia and get this all taken care of. You've already escaped the Frontier. They were destroyed back on Salt Crest."

I shook my head. *He has no idea what's on the way.*

Castin abruptly flipped the safety off his gun. "Hey! We've already been here! You leading us in circles?"

"No! I haven't! It just looks the same!" the Drifter protested.

"We've already been around this way. I saw that symbol earlier. I noticed 'cause the paint's all runny," Castin said, still pointing his gun at the Drifter's head. "Alright, that about does it here for you, I'd say."

"No! Wait! Don't shoot! Just let me lead the rest of the way! She's not far!" the stranger continued.

We all spoke quietly as he led us deeper into the trees, where the path began to clear. Snow started falling, and my stomach dropped as I realized we were walking into a deceitful ploy. My foot caught on a wire wrapped between two trees, and I grew dizzy with the realization. *We've been led into a trap! It's too late now!* A large gate swung closed behind us, and we were wrongfully shut in by the Frontier's security system.

The Drifter turned to us. "I had to do as I was told. I'm sure all of you can understand that in your own ways, right?"

An advancing blizzard began to swirl from the sweeping cold as we tried our best to avoid each other's glances. We soon saw two groups of Frontier members emerging from their building. Half were dressed in purple, the other gray, and they were armed with various elemental guns and swords.

One of them pointed directly at Zekiel, whose hair covered his face. The Librarian tightened the knot around his coat to hide his pockets, while Elijah desperately tried to wipe dried blood from his hands onto his pants. I held onto my rifle, with my sword sheathed. Castin tipped his dripping wet hat down, hiding a half-smile.

"Who's here?" a woman called out from inside.

Both sides exchanged glances, waiting for someone to respond, but all they got were confused shrugs.

The Drifter in front of us spoke loudly, "I have important information to share with you about them!"

I was then reminded of what the stranger heard earlier in the forest. *I know exactly what happens when word spreads. He knows that we were involved with F.E.M. He's going to tell them everything!*

A flash of light shot up from the ground next to us. Theia's silhouette came into view and stars fizzled around her as she teleported only a few steps from where we all stood. She greeted us simply, unsure of what to say as she seemed in awe to be using her powers, which was magnificent to witness up close.

"Up until now, I've only been able to teleport within a few feet of where I was. I don't know how far I can send all of us." Theia began trying to explain.

I caught her attention and mouthed the words *'again'* and *'you can do it'* while nodding to her finger. She closed her eyes and fell into a meditative state.

It was as if her powers were second nature, allowing her to maneuver away from the explosive boundary. Along with five others nearby, we were all transported to different rooms inside the building. A few individuals in purple and gray who had remained inside were the first to notice our sudden arrival.

They saw my group beginning to fight against attacks of their own, jumping in to defend without a second thought. It was usually those equipped with guns against anyone with swords, but now it was those in purple and gray facing off against the six of us, even though some of us were wearing their colors too.

A few members from both sides had sustained minor injuries—scrapes and bruises—as they leaped over brightly colored furniture while dodging attacks. Thankfully, there had been no deaths.

Then, quick footsteps echoed through the hallways, and everyone tensed, standing at attention.

We Magic Wielders held back from attacking as someone new, and evidently important, entered the room.

ELIJAH

Night

CHAPTER THIRTEEN: PAST EVENTS

"HISTORY HAS AN INTERESTING WAY OF repeating itself sometimes. But that's not always negative. Sometimes you're given a second opportunity to do things differently." Arcadia stood before all of us, her voice was as familiar as ever. It brought a sense of peace, a memory of simpler times.

My heart was racing as someone I thought I'd never see again singled me out from the crowd. *I must be chosen for a higher purpose. This is another sign. I can't deny what stands before me.* Her dark cloak swayed over the skin-tight modernistic suit beneath, a bold combination of purple and gray. The weapons she carried seemed to pulse with light, their magical and elemental properties glowing intermittently.

I'd never spoken to Arcadia, though I had always wanted to. Quietly, I wondered if she'd seen me at my town's falls when I'd carried out one last forced tragedy. Did she question whether I was part of the awful scene she had been investigating? *What does she know about the higher realm?* She was unforgettable.

And for some reason… it seemed that she also had her sights set on me. That was until Zekiel spoke up.

"What do you mean by 'doing things differently'?" he asked.

Arcadia's stare shifted to him. "Out of everyone, you have the most experience as a planetary fighter."

Zekiel kept his eyes forward, resisting the urge to look at anyone else who awaited his reaction. "I don't want to talk about the past," he replied.

"Time moves quite fast in those portals, doesn't it?" Arcadia continued. "In your memories, you recall stepping through the whimsical gateway, surrounded by swirling stars of various shapes and sizes. The anticipation of floating in nothingness, free from reality yet escaping what you thought was inevitable suffering and eventual death. A void you once knew was replaced with a different destination. One where magical seeds were planted over the years you drifted in a hypnotic state. You landed near the gray, muddy ghost town that became Salt Crest City after many years."

"Wait..." Zekiel took a deep breath. "Several *years* have passed?"

Arcadia was fighting off tears with a subtle crack in her tired voice. "Yes. I figured it was time you knew."

My temperature rose as her attention shifted to me. "Elijah. I'm finally getting to meet you. You took away my partner in crime."

"I... didn't do that on purpose." I struggled to suppress the flashbacks of abducting the woman she worked with. "I was forced."

Theia looked at me with guilty eyes. "You know I never wanted any of this to happen."

"Neither did I," Arcadia replied. "But here we are. The thing about reality is that it must be faced, regardless of how we feel. We move forward because time isn't going to wait for us. Alright? I can imagine it may be tough for some of us to be in this room together right now, but our feelings need to be shared later. Or never. I have instructions to give to you all."

"Wait…" I raised my hand towards her. "What do you know about me?"

"More than you'd expect, Cloudburst." She unfortunately didn't hold eye contact for long.

No one calls me by that name anymore. I fell silent. *I need to ask her more in private.*

Arcadia turned to Tule. "You've changed your stance."

Tule, who still had her sword sheathed, also held a polished chrome rifle. "I had no other choice. It was about survival," she explained.

"We'll go over the consequences of that choice later," Arcadia said, her posture stiffening. "We don't have time right now. I need to prepare you all for a new, very specific purpose. You're needed for a unique set of daring missions. The type of magic you possess can only be faced by seasoned Magic Wielders. Your experience is crucial."

"Don't tell me you're going to regroup us," Castin said, his voice laced with frustration. "Don't do this, alright? We've been through enough. I stick with my crew. That's how it is. I officially quit. Not sure if that's obvious enough by now, but I'm done. Take my title."

"You *know* you can't leave, Castin. Be careful what you do next," Arcadia warned. "All of you need to disperse to either side. We're starting with a high-priority task. Detailed instructions will be provided on-site."

Castin fell silent, tipping his head down and joining the others in gray without further discussion. Tule went over to the same group as him, and my eyes immediately landed on Zekiel to see how he would react. He looked taken aback as he saw her being handed a set of armor to change into, matching those who opposed their values.

"Really?" he asked, unable to hide the obvious and disappointed frown on his face.

She bit her lip and looked away. "I have no choice."

Zekiel refused to part with the sword I had given him. "I'm going with the Experiment Sciences group."

Tule remained quiet as Zekiel turned to join the others with no further discussion or hesitation. She looked equal parts pleased and worried by his decision, unsure if he understood the potential consequences of his last-second actions.

Theia, the Librarian, and I understood that we had no choice but to select a group as all eyes eventually turned to us. We joined the Experiment group, where the only familiar face was Zekiel. Each of us was given new attire and directed to different areas. A team of Frontier members kept a close watch over us, acting as security for the agency, always on high alert for any unexpected arrivals—or for hazardous threats they had created but couldn't control.

Every wall was white, so bright that it was hard to see with the lights covering almost every inch of the ceiling. We newcomers were directed to the changing rooms first, after walking through the disinfecting stations.

I took off my armor for the first time in a while. My muscles were sore, and I still felt like I was in fight-or-flight mode. I placed the black leather set into deep sanitized bins that were lined up for us on trays.

I was the last in line, and Arcadia saw it as an opportunity to pull me aside. I caught her out of the corner of my eye, motioning towards a nearby room. No one questioned me as I stepped away; Theia was in front of me but seemed not to notice that I had left her and the rest for a little while.

The small room was warm when I stepped inside, and Arcadia quickly closed the door behind me. It was cramped as we shuffled side to side.

"There's nowhere else we can talk right now without cameras or hidden microphones," Arcadia said worriedly. "We don't have much time, so please listen about where I came from and the role I play. If you remember only one thing from this conversation... Please let it be that not everything is the truth."

What should I say? I was at a loss for words for a second with her near me. "You work for the Frontier?"

Arcadia gave me a professional smile. "That's what they want you to think. Look around. Almost everyone is being controlled by someone else, or someone is attempting to control them. There are higher powers at play, Elijah—forces of nature we can't hope to face. The destruction of Salt Crest City, the plagues, and the storms that eroded its occupants and history were only the beginning. The solar system is at stake."

As I listened to her speak, I saw my mesmerized expression in the standing mirror behind her, along with how good the rest of her outfit looked. It took me a second to respond. "What are you telling me?"

"Question everything when you get there," Arcadia advised.

Suddenly, someone knocked on the changing room door. "Who is in here? There's no number hanging outside."

"I'll be out in one second," Arcadia called out.

"Oh... I'm so sorry to have interrupted you, Arcadia." Then, the stranger's footsteps faded away.

"What else do I need to know?" I asked once it was safe to do so.

"The original site of Crow Library was destroyed—a tragic loss of so many valuable books. However, second copies remain in *Old* Crow Library, buried under the mud. They contain some of the most important knowledge we have in this universe." She tapped her foot on the ground faster with each word.

"How are we supposed to preserve them?" I asked. "I've heard that those tunnels are infested with bloodthirsty psychopaths called Drifters, and worse, if you can believe it. I haven't ever been down there and don't want to go." I said, reaching for the doorknob, but her gentle touch stopped my hand.

"Would you do it if I told you that you're a chosen one?" she asked.

Another knock on the door made my heart skip a beat. "It's Elijah's turn now, Arcadia have you seen him around anywhere?"

I didn't respond to her before following the instructions after being questioned. As I left, she gave me an endearing look that lingered in my mind.

It only took a few minutes to get changed. I knew they wouldn't let me keep the legendary armor I had on after getting it back; they took it away, and I don't know where it went. We quickly followed orders to speed up the process, an uncomfortable dance between imbalances of power that I was already familiar with.

Almost everyone managed to keep the weapons they arrived with, except for Tule, who had to hand over her sword—an expensive piece she had purchased with a large savings of bay dollars.

The Librarian was publicly questioned about what was taking him so long in the changing rooms.

Someone knocked on the door. "Hey! You need to move faster! Our mission starts in fifteen minutes!"

"I-I... okay, sorry. Please hold on," he stammered.

"Why are you taking so long?"

He opened the door, dressed in the futuristic-looking armor in shades of purple that he was given. Though, he had covered most of it with his black coat, with only a hint of violet peeking through. *Was he wearing contacts earlier?* His eyes were brown.

"Why do you still have that on?"

"It's really important to me," the Librarian said, his voice resolute. "It has sentimental value. It's been passed down through generations in my family. I'm not going to lose it."

The masked stranger looked at Arcadia, who nodded. "Alright, you can keep it, but let me check it first."

The Librarian raised his hands as his attire was inspected for hidden items. I watched in disbelief as he seemed calm, not at all stressed despite the risks.

"Okay, he's good. Let's get moving."

After the guard moved away, the Librarian checked that his book was still securely tucked in its place. His fingertips touched the cloth binding, and he seemed to relax, assured it was still there. Then, he proudly showed the command that was written once out of view of the guards:

F.E.M.: HideInventory (MaxDuration)

"At least this place is a step up from where we came from," Castin said to Tule, who was nervously gearing up with ammo and a few other guns.

His voice was partly drowned out by the murmurs of everyone else around us, several pointing at signs to guide us newcomers to where we would rest for the night. There were instructions to 'input all information before entering sleep' and that 'once the screen locks, re-accessing the online portal is idle until morning'.

Each group was separated into different halves of the building to stay in when not on a mission. The rooms we were given had bunk beds, thick mattresses, lights, and a few dressers. In the top drawers, we found a pearly white tablet with rounded corners. The Librarian was the first from our group to find and examine it. Gently tapping the glossy black screen, it lit up immediately with a message:

WELCOME

TAP AGAIN TO ACTIVATE

He followed the on-screen instructions until prompted to scan his face and fingerprints. The device wouldn't let him proceed to the next step until he did, so he hesitantly began inputting key markers of his identity. Once all required information was collected, the Frontier's digital device finally allowed him to progress to the main menu to see what the Experiment Sciences operation would entail.

I walked a few hallways down where Tule was logging on with backup credentials. She was visiting the room Castin was sent to. "What are you doing?" he asked, watching as she operated the device. "Do I need to log on too with that other one over there?"

"Yes, but it would be great if you didn't need to," Tule replied.

"Have to do what's needed to survive," Castin said, extending his hand to take the tablet. "I don't have the energy to be a rule breaker right now. Trust me, I've got enough trouble coming my way from my past."

Tule refused. Instead, she retrieved her new silenced pistol, took the safety off, and pointed it at the screen.

"What are you doing?" he asked.

"Not letting them get access to you, too," she said confidently. The bullet went straight through the back of the advanced tech and into the top of the wooden dresser. "I'll tell them it was an accident."

"Never thought I'd see you do that." He stated in a supportive tone. "Wonder what the next step is to get out of this trap?"

Tule glanced at him, standing across from her in matching gray. "We'll see when we get there. Wherever they're sending us, I don't think Theia can teleport anyone much farther than she's shown."

I have to find out what it is we're going to have to do. Quietly, I went to my room to sleep for the night—well, to get as much rest as possible. On the way, I noticed mission purpose statements mounted on the walls:

ATTENTION ALL STAFF

Please familiarize yourself with the statements below and be sure to share no information publicly.

Our Boundaries:

Their purpose is to separate different regions of Earth, and other planets, from one another where conflicting magic must remain separate. Portals are only to be used for mission entry, all other forms of travel are prohibited, and discussing them is strongly discouraged.

Our Weapons:

Upon completion and enforcement of the Frontier's confidential weapons sanction, Euphrasia and Cyorio manufacturers retracted their wet and digital signatures on every prior agreement and arrangement for all bartering shops statewide. Emergency Biohazard personnel are to only use registered Cyorio Firearms weapons. Experiment Sciences personnel are to only use registered Euphrasia Arms weapons.

Please Remember:

Breaking these laws may result in portal disappearances, complete loss of all awareness in a sensory deprivation void, or death. We are not liable for any possible outcomes if personnel have misused these gateways or failed to follow law-enforced protocols.

Needless to say, I didn't get any sleep that night. I found myself wandering the halls, sidestepping sleep-deprived security guards. Theia and I crossed paths near a hallway dedicated to certain staff, adorned with plaques, awards, and informative statements hanging on the walls.

She was still wearing the same clothes as earlier, with her braids loose and a thick hair tie snugly around her right wrist. I noticed a mini notebook in her hand, with a word on the front:

EUPHRASIA

"Hey. Do you mind if we have a quick word?" I asked, stopping her as she was about to walk past me.

"We may end up on different sides here, but I think we can still talk."

The rows of circular lights above us had been dimmed but were still bright enough for me to see beads of sweat rolling down her face.

"I can't believe we're running into each other right now," Theia said, locking eyes with me. "You, of all people."

"Why? What's going on? I think we need to talk about what happened earlier. What we've endured together."

"We went through a harrowing ordeal when we weren't ourselves. Please call it what it was," Theia said.

"You brought me to you. You saved my life. Sometimes I try to tell myself that I don't care about you, did you know that? I try to convince myself of a reality that's not real so I can still function day to day. I want to believe it was just about the magic, but it all had to mean something."

I closed my eyes as my voice began to tremble. For a moment, I was back in a place I remembered too well. Theia stood before me with wonder and whimsical grace, as I was teleported to a place where our bond of loyalty was tested. She needed my assistance in more ways than one and was desperate to be set free after she had done the same for me. *I'll never be able to pay you bac—*

"You have it wrong!" Theia's voice rose. "That's not how it was, and you know it deep down! W-what we went through, what we did, we weren't our true selves."

"You can still hear my thoughts? Did you lie to me earlier when you said you couldn't?" I felt my stomach plummet.

"No! We're just on the same page!" Theia said.

"How can I ever trust you?" I knew I wouldn't be able to, but still wanted to know what her response was going to be.

"Who says you need to? I never asked for you to follow me! I didn't want you to come through that portal to rescue me!"

"So, when you fell into the tunnel... you didn't want me to save you?" I asked.

She didn't answer.

"Our past means nothing to you?"

"You don't even know all of it," she said.

"Excuse me?" I was almost left speechless.

"It turns out I didn't either," she replied, holding up the book. "I'd say more, but I'm afraid I can't. Not out loud, at least. You should read it for yourself, but it may get you killed. Don't say I didn't warn you."

She placed it into my hands and left in tears.

I was torn between wanting to hug her and pushing her away; for the past to be undone. I was reluctant to read the book I'd been given. *I wonder if she got this from the Old Crow Library? What could be in here? Do I even want to know? Will I regret finding out?* Regret would be difficult to face, but I had survived it before.

I headed to the nearest bathroom to read the first few pages, a place where I knew I wouldn't be recorded. Nothing could have prepared me for what I had been given—limitless and invaluable knowledge, and detailed descriptions and drawings that were made by Arcadia, a founder of the Frontier.

ENTRY ONE, Month: July. Day: Unknown

Hi to whoever from the other side is reading this. I know it's not anyone fully human because these pages should be burnt shortly after I'm done writing. I guess I don't have to be anonymous now. I have to admit it all.

Let's start at the falls. I unintentionally formed a mixture that caused a lot of deaths. I made many mistakes, but this was the worst of them all. Something that haunts me despite how much damage control I've tried to do. That's putting it all very simply, but it's far from that in my head. Every day I live with the truth.

I found out in the worst possible way that magic was within me. I'd gotten involved with powers I didn't know, or understand, when I unknowingly formed what has now become a boundary-enforcing agency that's taking over every state. I should've read the fine print before I drank the poison, took the medications I was told would help me by money-hungry doctors, and signed on as a founder.

Destruction. Chaos. I can hardly write as memories plague my mind of what's gone wrong. Especially at a waterfall where I tried to leave the substances that were controlling my life behind. A bout of regret traveled up my throat as I tried to relax and look at where the first portal was made.

"Why? Why is this all happening?" I asked out loud. "What have I done? What did I create? Such a mistake! Everything! Myself! I hate myself!"

I went behind the falls and got sprayed by the misty droplets that were carried my way by the wind. Everywhere I looked I could see caution tape and the remains of what was left of countless crime scenes.

In one hand I held onto my previous partner, Amira's, camera that she lost after getting abducted. In the other I held onto my bottle I found practically empty once returning to where I'd left it behind.

"This is all my fault!" I yelled and threw it against the rocks without a second thought.

I didn't realize at the time that I had made everything far, far worse. The cracked glass flew everywhere upon impact and a couple of shards landed in my eyes. At first, it made it hard for me to see the remnants of the dark red and magenta-colored drink that had made its way into the rushing waters.

The curse spread as it entered a vulnerable stream. That's when another portal formed. I had trembled in terror as I watched it appear and had to choose whether or not to go inside.

I wondered, what if this is my only chance to fix everything? To make things right? What if this is how I can go save all of these people and correct my mistakes?

It began closing with only seconds left for me to make my choice. So, I stepped in at the last moment. That's when I entered through Euphrasia's gates, one of the most utopian places I'd ever encountered. The city was home to several towering buildings, virtual billboards, and advanced technology that I'd only seen in films.

Futuristic fighters waited patiently there for someone to lead them. I wasn't sure how long they'd been there, but it was enough for them to be expertly trained. They had prepared specialized guns and swords for whatever was to happen next.

Nero and those he led had their plans ready.

I'll save the following events that took place for my next entry, but wanted to include some poems that I wrote during that time to end this one:

I Made My Choice
I won't hesitate,
To train again and again.
I'll help those I trust.

Flower
A fire that ignites,
Green anxiety burning.
Energy transformed through smoke,
Let the medicine fill your lungs.
Inhale the healing,
Exhale the damage.
Embrace the high,
It will never end.
To the orange and blue hues,
Flexible and burning fervently.
Button pressed and lighter in position,
Sideways flame.

I Saw Everything

I know the power that abuse held over you,

Cursed under someone else's control.

You thought there was no escape,

It turned out there was, yet you ran from that too.

Unable to ask for help,

Worried about what they'd think of you.

During the hot quiet night,

Something doesn't feel quite right.

How turning off the light,

Might make terrors come to life.

If in the middle of the darkness,

I hear my doorbell ring,

Yet no one was expected to be visiting.

—Arcadia

ZEKIEL

Morning-Evening-Morning

CHAPTER FOURTEEN: WIELDERS OF MAGIC

IT WAS A FREEZING COLD MORNING AS

snow fell, blanketing the pine trees' fading dark green leaves. A new type of season had arrived, foreshadowing the upcoming challenges and otherworldly terrors we would soon face. The forest was dense and confusing, with certain trees spray-painted with different markings. Some of them were hidden, but most were easy to see in the daylight as we traveled on foot. Those of us within the

Frontier's boundary didn't stay there long, as our missions were about to begin in an hour.

I was grateful to have Tule by my side despite everything that had happened. I wasn't sure we'd survive the mist storms, the mutants, or the magnetic countdown. I always enjoyed her company and friendship, but I also wanted space. I found it easy to hide my emotions from those around me.

I need her to know that I'm all in. That I'll work with whatever magic I have to in order to ensure our safety. She has to know that she can rely on me. Even though we're now standing on opposite sides, she seems to understand my choice. Hopefully this will blow over soon.

Everyone under the highly enforced supervision of the Frontier was geared up and on the way to each upcoming mission. My skin stung in the cold, and hair was secured behind me in a tight bun. It felt burdensome picking up my feet in the snow while progressing on.

"I feel like I recognize this place from somewhere." The Librarian spoke up in the middle of the group.

I rubbed my hands together to keep them warm. Snowflakes fell on our hats, masks, and bare faces, tiny speckles landing delicately on my eyelashes.

"Same here," I replied with a nod and inhaled deeply, "Reminds me of a book Tule showed me. The tunnels below must've been what the title was referring to." *Why was that 'X' marked on the map?*

Armed personnel from the agency began paying more attention to what was being said, so we held our tongues. The only sound for a while was of others' voices, speculating on the day's challenges based solely on their previous deadly excursion.

As we reached our wintry checkpoint, the snowfall intensified. Our matching purple outfits were quickly covered in snowflakes, and my teeth began chattering in the blistering cold. The location for the other assignment that Tule and Castin were on was near ours. Their group walked at the same brisk pace as we did in the opposite direction. Elijah, Theia, the Librarian, and I stayed close together as we entered unknown terrain and watched each other's backs.

The crew that was sent to oversee our work wore black stripes on their arms and were the only ones with what appeared to be walkie-talkies on their waistbands. Each had an antenna and speakers that probably transmitted live feedback of our conversations. It was then that I decided to be even more careful with my words. *So, they're all listening to us too?* I kept mostly silent as the others spoke nearby.

"Good call with the coat earlier," Theia said.

The Librarian responded, "Thank you."

She continued, "No, thank *you* for everything you've done throughout this journey. We couldn't have made it here without you."

"Ah well, just helping where I can," he said modestly. "Like working at the Sea Bartering shop."

Theia sounded impressed, "That's some honest work, helping out in a place like that with no hope in exchange for lost time. Seems it would get daunting."

"The bay dollars were worth it," the Librarian said, "But honestly... I just enjoyed helping out. I like to be there for others in some way. If I'm not working, well, I'd be reading or writing in the library while smoking the largest joint I could roll."

"The more I talk to you, the more you remind me of Tule. You both would really get along," Theia said.

I looked up from the ground at the unexpected mention of her name as we continued through the chilling morning. *She asked him to help heal me. I wonder what they spoke about when I wasn't there?*

"A few others have told me that too. She appeared to be interested in my books. You know, I wonder how many times she was at the library at the same time as me and I had no idea. Two different sides of the same shelf." The Librarian couldn't refrain from smiling with his next words, "I just met her recently. I'd heard of her before, seen her around. How could I miss her beauty? Everything I heard is true. She seems to be amazing. People like her are the best—those who also enjoy learning new things and have a desire to share that knowledge. Wanting to do right by others."

"What about Castin? What was your experience with him before we arrived?" Theia asked curiously.

"Distant," the Librarian replied. "He rejected all notions and conversations about magic for a while. When I first met him, I thought, 'ah, this guy is a Magic Wielder hater', you know the type. Turns out he's one of us. It's interesting, yet sad, how so many people want nothing to do with others who have things in common with them. Surrounding yourself with those who mirror you can sometimes lead to uncomfortable self-reflection that's easier to avoid."

Theia and Elijah fell silent for a few moments.

"I remember how Castin didn't want to hear anything I had to say when we first met," the Librarian elaborated further. "He perpetuated the same type of problematic thinking that most of the citygoers had—an unwillingness to understand the unseen. And then he surprised me by joining the rescue search in the tunnels. He shockingly chose to suppor—" The Librarian suddenly became very silent.

"You okay?" Elijah asked.

Theia's face creased with worry. "What's wrong?"

"Am I saying too much?" the Librarian asked, his voice uncertain. "I'm sorry if I'm talking a lot. I didn't realize until now just how many thoughts I have bottled up inside. Like a bottle of ink filled with words waiting to be written. I need to finally release them."

"Makes sense," Elijah replied with a nod. "I'd have a lot to say too if I didn't share what's going on inside my head with someone."

Theia changed the topic. "Did you read about our mission? I forgot to ask earlier how you managed to get that tablet to work without help from the staff."

The Librarian cleared his throat. "It said we're going to the volcanoes. Experiments gone wrong, some type of threatening mutants, are wreaking havoc that they need us to eradicate."

As we reached our destinations, the gap between our two groups grew wider. We were covered in snow, and our boots left indents in it with every uniform step. I longed to return to the Frontier Headquarters. Despite the coldness of those there, the building was at least warm, and we had access to an unlimited supply of food, drinks, and almost anything else we needed.

"How much of the statement do you remember exactly?" I finally spoke up to ask him and the Librarian showed us the notes he had written down:

EXPERIMENT SCIENCES

Location: Mud Volcanoes

Difficulty: Recommended M.lvl: 30

About: Failed experiments are roaming the volcanic ruins and will soon reach the town of Magma if not destroyed.

Objective: Eradicate volcanic mutants.

Tule recalled her main instruction to me earlier before we parted ways, so I knew what she would be facing:

EMERGENCY BIOHAZARD

Location: Magma Town

Difficulty: Recommended M.lvl: 20

About: Town members are trapped under pieces of planetary mass after a sudden volcanic eruption.

Objective: Extricate victims from hazardous rubble.

Theia, Elijah, the Librarian, and I approached our site with bated breaths and equipped weapons. We stayed towards the back of the group, who were already entering the mud volcanoes. However, we initially kept our distance to see what would happen.

The first things that came into view were the bubbly mud pots. There was a long stretch of gray mud off the path of forest trees as we ventured from safer grounds. The piles of mud grew higher as I watched the others navigate around the sinkholes. They began at ankle height, then reached our knees, and eventually our waists. Soon, we'd ventured deep enough into the new terrain that they towered over our heads.

Visibility became limited. "Why didn't the packet say what the creatures look like?" Someone pulled out a set of binoculars to get a better view while climbing atop a massive pile that slowly began to rise, the mound eventually revealing itself as one of them.

"Everyone, over here!" Elijah called as he drew his sword.

The woman cried out for help as she brandished a short blade, one that would be inadequate for the terror she faced. This mutant stood tall on four legs and resembled a rhinoceros. As it stirred, it grew angry, kicking at the mud and charging forward. Cracks started appearing in its rough skin, exposing orange and yellow bubbles, dripping out of the opening like honeyed lava. As she clung to the creature's back, the substance burned her fingers. Her allies tried attacking one of its legs as it shook the ground, but other horrors that had been sleeping nearby were also awakened and began fleeing from the experimenters and fellow fighters.

"I don't think that they are hostile!" Theia yelled. "They don't want to harm us! Let's leave them alone!"

"We have to follow orders!" a stranger replied.

The woman in the stressful situation was then kicked off as the intimidating variant charged to join the others heading towards Magma Town.

Everyone ran after them with their swords drawn, except for the crew members who had stayed on the outskirts of the site to act as backup. Five of those waiting for orders were trampled and killed as the chaos unfolded.

"We have to keep moving!" Theia's hands trembled as she neared Elijah. "How are we expected to do this without guns? I don't have any throwables with me!"

The Librarian, not far behind them, said, "We need to hurry and warn the others! That's the direction they're heading in! That's where Tule and Castin are!"

The mutants bulldozed through the vegetation, knocking down any trees in their path. Screams of terror rang out as they approached our opposing site, which resembled a crime scene. Pieces of planetary debris were scattered around, volcanic ash covered the damaged houses, and specks of lava singed at the ground. Our group had managed to save most of those trapped under the hot, sharp rubble and were being tended to. Most of the burn victims' wounds needed immediate attention with the portable health kits.

However, our progress was at risk of being undone as nearby creatures barreled through the wreckage, threatening the already fragile state of the injured.

More were trampled.

Screams multiplied and grew louder.

Shots started firing.

Tule needed to reload. She had to be careful not to miss as the onlookers in purple watched in worry.

Once most of the experiments were dead, they began assisting in cleaning up what they could with specialized tools intended for the remains.

By the end of our mission gone wrong, just over twenty lives had been lost in the unpredictable ordeal. We, the Magic Wielders, had survived the messy events from both sides, and then we began seeking each other out to ensure we were all still alive.

Arcadia rallied up the high-ranking members of the Frontier to discuss what would happen next based on the day's upcoming, and most likely dire, events.

Medical staff were nearby to transport the remaining survivors from Magma Town to their base, for what I assumed would be secret trials and hidden plans of experimentation. We dusted ourselves off, stretched, and some of the others leaned on each other for support as the afternoon approached.

"There's something we need to discuss." I pointed towards my chest where Castin had stabbed me, interrupting his conversation with someone else. "You have to promise never to attack nor threaten Tule or me again. If we don't stick together, everything will fall apart, alright? I've seen and experienced that firsthand. Everyone turns against one another, with mistrust and half-truths. I refuse to walk with someone I have to keep a watchful eye on due to disloyalty."

"You know why I did that," Castin grunted, rolling his shoulders. "Was a misunderstanding. Right, Tule?"

"It was," Tule agreed as she heard everything we were talking about, "I promise. I was forced to do what I did. The Frontier threatened to go after my fami—"

"I need everyone to gather around," Arcadia cut off her sentence, uneasily watching us huddle together.

Many wiped sweat and blood from their foreheads while trying to avoid looking at the corpses scattered around. The wind stung the faces of those of us without masks.

"We have a new mission for you," Arcadia announced, "This will be unlike anything you've faced before." She pulled her black velvet gloves on tighter, her hood keeping most of her face covered. "The tasks ahead require us to modify our standard approach."

"How about you send some of us back home? There's no way you need all of us," Castin suggested.

"You're partly right," she replied.

I held my breath in excited anticipation.

"So… you'll let us go?" Castin asked, his expression skeptical of how her words were too good to be true.

"Those of you below magic level twenty, yes. We'll have to let you go. Staff will ensure you go through the necessary cleansing steps needed for release."

I'm not sure if I'm below or past that. I grew anxious.

Elijah, whose short braids were covered in snow, looked the most confused. "I don't understand…"

Arcadia approached with her arms crossed, her sleeves adorned with symbols. "Both sides will be coming together, but that alone won't be enough, not for what's ahead. There are specific locations that must be seized from an organization that has gotten a hold of our magic. Each location requires different mastery, experience, and knowledge in specific areas of the realm. Everything can become destroyed when the wrong influences get involved. If you truly care about saving others and ensuring freedom for your future, you will confront them all under my monitored help."

"But *you're* the Frontier, Arcadia. I know you don't play an innocent role in any of this," Castin spouted.

"You're confusing us with the F.E.M. corporation, we're very separate," Arcadia explained. "The difference between us? We let you walk away after you've stepped foot into our territory, meddled with our magic, played by the rules. But F.E.M.? That's an eternity, for life, sort of thing. They want souls. If any of you have used or accepted help from that type of magic unknowingly... I don't really know what to say."

"How are you breaking up this huge group of us?" I asked before the realization dawned on me. *Oh.*

Arcadia took a step back. "Can all the wielders of magic please step forward?"

Tule, Theia, Elijah, Castin, the Librarian, and I stepped away from the rest, our footprints side by side in the snow.

"You will each lead a team consisting of members from both groups," she announced authoritatively.

"You're separating us?" I asked worriedly as I looked over at Tule.

"We're instructed to," Arcadia said. "But by now, you should be seasoned professionals, right? I'm sure you'll all see each other again after this gets taken care of. Some of you may have to be paired off, though."

"What can you tell us about the sites?" Elijah asked.

"Each has practiced planetary magic and activated nuclear threats, spellbinding curses, and unfathomable terror from the darkness. What they've done depends on the type of Forced Evolutionary Magic that they've used. The six of you have remarkable skills that let you assist in a way that no one else can. You'll find out more soon. In fact, you will... *be* there soon."

The challenges we had overcome thus far had prepared us for the new ones that superseded even our wildest imaginations.

I looked down at my hands.

Castin examined his tattoos.

Tule glanced over at the nearby greenery.

Theia and Elijah, their right pointer fingers.

The Librarian held a hand over his book and tools.

The snow fell harder, making everything slippery. Then, a loud crack echoed as one of his bottles slipped onto the ground from his coat, interrupting the silence as it broke, and its contents had spilled near all of our feet.

The sound of that glass cracking was deafening.

An iridescent ink simmered and melted a patch of pure white snow that surrounded the town. The other Magic Wielders and I received judgmental looks from those wearing matching uniforms. The existence of our supernatural abilities had been pushed to the forefront of everyone's minds as Arcadia drew as much attention to them as possible.

The Librarian's nerves seemed to be catching up with him. The ink had splashed onto his fingers and across the bottoms of his pant legs and shoes. We observed the costly mistake until something else caught my attention nearby. A militant group dressed in jet black emerged from the sidelines. Each member was equipped head to toe with futuristic gear, durable armor, and matching assault rifles. They appeared to be an extension of the crew that was with us earlier.

One of them walked in front of the rest as they got closer, making hand gestures toward the six of us. Another handed a device to Arcadia with a curt nod, the piece of equipment resembling a metal baton that had a large gray button. As they drew nearer, I was able to read the name painted on their plastic shields:

THE SECOND CREW

"Its operation steps are the same as the others. We can explain the process to them while on the way," one of the newcomers said.

Arcadia looked at him from beneath her snowy red bangs. "Thanks."

"No. Thank *you* for alerting us to their arrival. We needed this help more than ever," he replied. "Things there are currently a free-for-all and it's getting worse."

"Do you think they will survive what's to come?" She crossed her arms and frowned while asking.

"What?" The man's voice dropped to a whisper. "Why would you ask that? Putting up a front or something? You know where the trip ends, right? Doubt they'll feel anything at all."

Arcadia bit her bottom lip, her silence speaking volumes.

Castin took off his hat and smirked. "You guys talking about us, or?"

"Just going over some final details. I have to get this projector bar ready," Arcadia said as she held it up. "The six of you are leaving with them and the rest of us will remain at the Frontier's headquarters. Your mission is going to be broadcast for us to watch."

"What can you tell us?" Elijah inquired, giving her a reassuring look.

"Each location holds a key to the next. Once you get to it, you have to share it so another can begin seizing their assigned location as you complete your own mission. A relay race of sorts, passing a baton, but every second counts differently in this case. It will take time to get through where you're going and the hordes you'll be fighting off. By the time you make it to the middle, the next locations will already be in progress. You should all make it to the end of each compound around the same time."

After that, we were integrated into the serious yet friendly group of new arrivals that looked us up and down with caution. They were already aware of our rare abilities, tools, and weaponry—things I had once wished to never have. Though, I wouldn't have come as far as I had without them.

My focus lingered on those standing beside me, dressed in lavender and stormy gray. None of them spoke as we were scrutinized by many unknown armed personnel.

We soon left Magma Town, and the lava-stained, mangled mess, with the Second Crew. Our trails of patterned boot marks pressed into the snow.

One of the strangers told us, "It'll be about a forty-five-minute drive from here."

We traveled through the bulk of the forest, past the most congregated area of pine trees. Our conversation was minimal; we wanted to be extra careful with what we shared while surrounded by the watchful strangers.

"The smell of their terpenes is stronger than usual," Tule remarked. "It's as if their chemical compounds have been altered or evolved in some way before evaporating."

"I was thinking the same thing," the Librarian agreed.

"Smells the same to me," Castin grunted.

Beyond the unusual trees were the crew's camouflage-wrapped vehicles. They were large four-wheelers that came equipped with nearly indestructible turrets, bulletproof tinted windows, and ample space filled with resources. Each vehicle was electric and made hardly any sound as they drove, giving the sensation of floating.

I fastened my seatbelt. Tule and the Librarian were seated in the front, while Theia, Elijah, and Castin occupied the back row with me. We were transported along the unfamiliar snowy roads, and the morning turned to afternoon as most of us remained quiet.

The vehicle grew colder with each mile, and I rubbed my hands together again for warmth. The wind pushed against us, the trees on either side swaying violently. I felt a sense of despair watching them, knowing many were just seconds away from destruction—stuck in the oncoming and harsh storm.

"Do any of you have questions for us?" asked the stranger operating the vehicle as we sped along. "We're sure you have many, just as we once did."

I kept my eyes on the window beside me and tampered with the nearest buttons to see which one could roll it down. "I only have one. What's the name of this place?"

"Metal Island," came the reply.

No one else asked anything after we learned our destination.

A woman sitting in the front row passed back six manila packets. "Here you go."

They bore no letters or numbers on the front, only a label on the back that stated:

F.E.M. BOUNDARY HUNTER

The sticky seal at the envelope's opening was covered with layers of green tape. *Who messed with this?* It took me a few moments to peel it away without ripping the fragile contents inside. I found three sheets of the thinnest paper I'd ever felt tucked tightly into the envelope. I grabbed the stack by its left side and held it up to the window, allowing the sunlight to illuminate the instructions. As the pages started to fall, I carefully held the top right corner to keep them in place.

The words were stacked on top of one another, each layer obscuring the text on the pages beneath it. Frustrated, I was about to put two pages back into the envelope to examine them one at a time...

Until I noticed something.

A Drifter's symbol was marked in the bottom right corner of the page, stamped with a fading special ink.

I heard the two at the front of the vehicle fall into a stressed argument. "Hopefully you gave him the *correct* one, Arcadia was very adamant about that."

Their whispers could easily be heard during the quiet drive. I kept my head down, though, and refrained from displaying any reaction to their words.

"I'm sure I did. Why? What's making you worried?" One of the strangers in front of me asked.

"I mean... he's holding pages up to the window." The other responded in a frustrated and gritty tone. "That better not be something made by Glass."

I continued to read and study all that I could, despite the murmured exchange up front. Little graffiti symbols were scattered all over the front and back of each page—clouds, and more clouds. The more I looked, the more I found.

The hairs on my arms stood up as I recalled similar markings in the forest. The smell of fresh paint lingered in the air; each marking had been recently sprayed at the base of many trees. The sheer number of them seemed endless, each with a different size and style, indicating that no two were made by the same person.

The Drifters. I felt uneasy. *They're probably dropping us into a nest of them. We have to be ready for whatever is going to come next.*

We were getting closer to what ended up becoming our first 'checkpoint' as a light beam flashed and beeping came from the speakers. It was then we arrived at the entrance of Metal Island.

"Yeah, we know," the driver said as he tapped a glass button to turn the sound off.

The other Frontier vehicles beside and behind us came to a complete stop. We remained seated as the Second Crew hurriedly exited through all four doors. *Where are they running to?*

I glanced curiously out of the tinted windows and saw the giant metal fortress for the first time. It resembled a colossal silver grater, with blades jutting out from each hole. We couldn't see inside from where we were. Each side of the building had gates extending infinitely left and right. Near the main entrance were several holographic stations, activated by chips in the team's wristbands hidden underneath their sleeves.

What are they doing? I watched in confusion as they scanned one at a time. I thought they were going to unlock the door, but they didn't move towards it. Instead, they came back to the vehicle and sat down.

"Took too much time!" one of them chided.

"I could only drive so fast, okay? Speeding on this snow could have endangered everyone. There are too many blind spots coming out of that forest," the driver replied.

The strangers ran back to the vehicles, closed their doors, and started them up again, signaling for us to exit.

"Do we have to go to those stations too?" I asked.

"Yeah, to check in. Make sure you get to them quickly after you first punch in. Everything else will be explained as you continue. Thanks for complying;

many of the others have made the drive much worse than you. Every second counts, and borrowed time has to be earned."

The driver gave us wristbands. They were silver with adjustable clasps for comfort, but they felt extra cold to the touch. I noticed my initials engraved inside.

How do they know my last name? I pondered.

I inhaled deeply before putting it on, my breath visible in the snowy air as I exhaled. The wind was strong, and the dark purple armor I wore offered little warmth. The frigid metal slightly numbed my skin as I secured the band around my wrist, covered in goosebumps underneath all that I wore. *It's so cold.*

Once all of them were secured, they let out the same beeping noise that we heard upon entering. Three barely audible confirmation sounds followed. The automated tightening system made the metal cling to me with more pressure. I followed the others over to the station and waved my arm over it after everyone else had left. A little message popped up in a pixelated font on the top of the band.

1,800 SECONDS

...

1,799 SECONDS

...

1,798 SECONDS

The countdown continued. *Before what?* The station we just checked into had an introductory paragraph. The beginning of it read,

ATTN: EMPLOYEES

Every station is to be checked into by 7:00 P.M. If unable to meet your time mark, reach out to your supervisor with a thoroughly written explanation. We are not liable for any health-related causes (including, but not limited to): injury, unforeseen disappearances, or death. You are not to directly touch or interact with any elements of Forced Evolutionary Magic aside from the removal and extermination of it. Those discovered to have broken staff rules with F.E.M. will be subject to strict consequences determined on a case-by-case basis.

The final sentences were unreadable, covered by graffiti of Drifter symbols from the forest and phrases I'd also seen around Salt Crest City.

How have I never been told about this place?

My eyes drifted back to the tower. Snow had piled on the little ledges of metal that stuck out. I glanced down at my wristband again and tapped on it to see if anything else would happen.

A vehicle that closely resembled the one we'd been dropped off in pulled up a few feet from where we stood. There were no bushes, trees, or anything else to hide behind—just a tall, thin pole and the entrance nearby.

That's when Castin used his power to turn all six of us into shadowy figures. One hand was on his hat and the other one was extended towards me and the rest.

"No one say anything," he whispered and stayed still. "Don't move. Just wait until we see who it is."

"Where did you all go?" I heard Elijah ask.

Castin made sure to keep a hand up on the side of his hat, the brim collecting snow, until he deemed it safe to remove it. "We're all here. Just can't see each other."

The driver came to an abrupt stop and jumped out of the car once it was parked. A woman I'd never seen before, clad in thick armor, stepped into view. Her blonde ponytail, like the rest of her, was covered in snow. She opened the backseat door and motioned for someone to step outside.

"Please don't make this difficult, Glass. I'm just following orders; you know this isn't personal," she said.

She closed the door behind him after he exited. Both of them wore similar suits of leather, but his outfit had what looked to be bullet-proof glass incorporated throughout, revealing his pale skin. The falling snow blended in with his hair, and he pulled the woman into an embrace before parting ways.

"Make it back alive, okay?" she called behind him.

"There's no need to worry. I have this under control. We'll speak soon." He gave her a nod as she got back into the car and sped off. The man walked in a circle once she was gone. "Didn't think they'd ever find out. What now?" he asked himself aloud.

Castin let go of his hat and brought the group of us into view again. "He's wearing gray."

"Who's there?" The stranger turned around as we suddenly appeared and focused intently on all of us.

"We've been sent on a mission by Arcadia to seize locations. Apparently being timed," Castin pointed to his wristband. "Why? You sent here to help us or?"

"No. I have no idea about any of this. I recognize that device on your arm, though, what is it saying?" Glass walked close to the six of us to hear us better.

"**1,638**," I replied.

"You need to earn more time before it runs out," he responded with a hint of nervousness in his voice.

Once we all were scanned in, one of the huge doors on some sort of barrier opened, leading to the ocean. My eyes caught on the graffiti on the inside walls as we walked towards the water.

TRANSPARENCY IS KEY, USE IT WISELY

I couldn't help but read the words again:

TRANSPARENCY IS KEY, USE IT WISELY

On the mossy concrete, we looked over the edge where it dropped off into the waves and saw a boarding dock. Then a ship with its name on the side in royal blue cursive lettering:

THE END

NOVEL EXTRA: CHARACTER POEMS

ZEKIEL

The Fallout

No longer bound by the chains of a lonely hue,

Abandoning what I knew to embrace the truth.

A hidden symbol given power through who'll win,

A dystopian end now forms a future I see light in.

CASTIN

Snow-Filled Hat

With just the touch of a fingertip,

I'll make all of your worries fade away.

Unseen power is often the most misunderstood.

TULE

Beat the Clock

So much at stake when letting go of mistakes,

A lone wanderer with a heart full of wanderlust.

Many others believed I was losing my mind,

When really I was finding it just in time.

ELIJAH

Closure

I didn't mean what I said.

Were those words mine? Not sure.

Someone else was in my head.

THEIA

Advice

Is what was said true?
That I should be my own best friend?
Since enemies should be kept the closest?

THE LIBRARIAN

Page Turner

The storms of life almost overtook me,
Turning to an unforgiving world to fill a void.
Met with harsh realities and mundane routines,
I was desperate for escapism to the highest degree.
Pouring words on paper from a half-empty bottle,
Harnessing their power through therapeutic pleas.
Absolvement of guilt and misdirection saved me,
Faith in the unseen that words can't even express.
A discovered coin with value that never changes,
Two sides to the same antiquely treasured currency.
When I saw her I knew that one thing was true,
That I had to see what our next chapter held.
When she asked for help I was there for her,
Peacefulness hit harder than any drug ever could.

Time is always moving onwards as we do the same,
Only the words of truth can withstand its tests.